Review

ON

Union Station

EarthCent Ambassador Series:

Date Night on Union Station

Alien Night on Union Station

High Priest on Union Station

Spy Night on Union Station

Carnival on Union Station

Wanderers on Union Station

Vacation on Union Station

Guest Night on Union Station

Word Night on Union Station

Party Night on Union Station

Review Night on Union Station

Family Night on Union Station

Book Night on Union Station

LARP Night on Union Station

Book Eleven of EarthCent Ambassador

Review Night on Union Station

Foner Books

ISBN 978-1-948691-00-0

Northampton, Massachusetts

One

"In conclusion, it is the view of Union Station Embassy that the upcoming review of humanity's progress towards integration with the tunnel network will be a valuable opportunity to solicit guidance from the older species, especially those which generally hold themselves aloof from dealing with us outside of diplomatic contacts, and I fully expect a positive report."

Kelly inhaled and shook her head ruefully at her unintentional edit. She had planned to say something encouraging about how all of the alien businesses setting up shop on Earth in recent years were creating a small but effective pro-human lobby in some quarters. Unfortunately, it had slipped her mind after she began speaking, and she doubted her ability to include it in a new conclusion without forgetting something else.

"The purpose of our soliciting guidance from existing tunnel network members is to give them a chance to influence the decision process regarding your probationary status," Libby informed the ambassador.

Kelly reflexively glanced up at the ceiling before replying to the omnipresent Stryx librarian.

"I thought this whole review was just a formality, though to tell you the truth, I'm still a little fuzzy on what we would gain by getting off of probationary status and becoming full members. Jeeves already told me that Earth will remain a protectorate until we develop a self-defense capability."

"The primary benefit is access to certain information that is currently being withheld due to your probationary status."

"Such as?"

"I'm afraid that answer would fall within the domain of certain information that is currently being withheld due to your probationary status," Libby replied innocently.

"Sounds like a pig in a poke to me," Kelly grumbled. "Do you think I should be doing something to prepare for the review? It came up at our last intelligence steering committee meeting, but none of the other ambassadors had any ideas."

"There's really not anything you can do to prepare at this point."

"Are you implying that we could have done something if we started earlier?"

"Would you have grafted on two more arms to please the Dollnicks, or sprouted a tentacle to curry favor with the Drazens?"

"I guess not." Kelly began to push her chair back from the display desk, but changed her mind mid-action and returned to her original position. "Am I forgetting any-thing else? Didn't Donna ask me to do something before leaving? Maybe I should look over my calendar for the next few cycles."

"Are you that afraid to go home and face Dorothy?" Libby asked, her synthesized voice taking on a concerned tone.

"I know I'm being a bad mother but I just can't take it anymore. She's been willing herself to be miserable ever since David eloped with Hannah. It's not like he didn't ask Dorothy to marry him at least three times."

"It did seem to me that she was pushing the two of them together," Libby mused. "If Dorothy had been a client of my dating service, I would have stopped sending her serious prospects like David until she showed a willingness to commit."

"That's exactly what I mean. It's been three months already, and if she loses any more weight, she's going to be able to model her own clothes. David was a great guy, and I would have been happy to have him as a son-in-law, but who ever heard of finding a future husband in the lost-and-found?"

The Stryx librarian remained silent.

"Libby? Was the whole David thing one of your set-ups?"

"Brinda just entered the embassy," Libby announced. "No need to get up. I'll override the lock for you."

The door to Kelly's office slid open and four puppies, each of which was the size of a mature Great Dane, tried to enter at the same time, creating a jam. Then they burst through all at once, sprawling on the floor and rolling joyfully over one another. The younger Hadad sister followed them into the room.

"Is it that time already?" Kelly asked, surveying the rambunctious puppies with a combination of amusement and dismay.

"I wish we had room to keep them all, but the truth is we barely have space for Pava," Brinda said, referring to the female Cayl hound named after the emperor's wife. "We would have needed to farm them out cycles ago if Jeeves hadn't temporarily rented the apartment next to ours and put in a dog door to double our space."

"That was pretty nice of him."

"He said it was in the benefits section of my partnership agreement for SBJ Fashions and I didn't ask to read it. My sister's family has been adopted by the female, and one of the males took a fancy to Blythe's twins. She and Clive agreed to accept him on a trial basis, provided we give them a return option."

"Well, I suppose Beowulf will keep the last two in line until we find somebody they can respect. How did Pava react?"

"She chased them all out of the apartment five minutes ago. That's how I knew it was time. The Cayl have invested millions of years in breeding these hounds for military service, so they know their duty. Watch this."

Brinda clapped once, and the four puppies immediately stopped their frolicking and formed a row, sitting tall on their haunches.

"Who's going to Shaina?" Brinda asked. "Fall out and wait for me in the other room."

One of the puppies backed out of the row, gave each of her brothers a sniff to impress their scents on her memory, and then trotted out of Kelly's office without looking back.

"Which one of you picked Blythe's kids?"

The puppy on the end let its tongue loll out of its mouth, winked at the other two, and then followed his sister.

"We speak English to them all the time, so you shouldn't have any more trouble communicating than you do with Beowulf," Brinda explained.

"Which means they'll understand when they want to," the ambassador observed dryly. "Okay. I guess the two of you are coming home with me." Kelly eyed the puppies with trepidation, and they both gave her such innocent looks that she just knew they were going to be trouble.

"The house will feel pretty empty with only Pava left," Brinda remarked wistfully. The two women paused in the outer office, the puppies crowding around them.

"You still have Walter and the baby," Kelly reminded her. "Hey. Can I interest you in taking Dorothy off our hands? We'll pay room and board."

"I'd rather have all of the puppies back, even without the extra apartment space. Dorothy's driving us nuts at work on the odd days she actually bothers to come in. Last week I asked her what colors she wanted for the new prototypes, and she answered, 'What difference does it make? They're just shoes.'"

"She said what? I don't believe you. Shoes are her life."

"Affie and Flazint have both come to me separately to ask if there's anything they can do to help, but even though they're Dorothy's best friends, they have trouble under-standing what happened. Affie doesn't get why Dorothy is upset because David was just a—I can't remember her exact term, but it was a Vergallian word that implied a practice boyfriend about whom one feels possessive."

"That seems like a pretty accurate description."

"And Flazint keeps forgetting that Dorothy and David didn't have a negotiated companionship agreement, so she's always offering to go over the contract to check for violations."

"I'll talk to Dorothy again," Kelly replied with a sigh. "Maybe the puppies will cheer her up."

Brinda repressed a shudder on hearing Kelly's last three words. "Ugh. Did you know that Jeeves has been trying to cheer her up at work with his insane concept of humor? Trust me, you don't want examples."

5

The female Cayl hound whined and scratched at the floor, evidently in a hurry to move on to her new home. Both women were glad of an excuse to drop the conversation at that point, and they followed the puppies out of the embassy. The ambassador headed for the lift tube with the two she was bringing home, and Brinda strolled off in the opposite direction to drop off a puppy for the twins.

When Kelly exited the lift tube in the corridor outside of Mac's Bones, the two puppies immediately picked up Beowulf's scent and tore off in search of their father. The ambassador followed at a funereal pace, which seemed fitting given Dorothy's ongoing mourning over the loss of her practice boyfriend.

"Can we keep them?" Fenna asked excitedly. Kelly halted her slow march back to the scrapped ice harvester that served as the extended family home, happy for a reason to delay entering. Aisha's six-year-old daughter looked like a doll next to the giant puppies, which were being careful not to knock her down in their frolicking. "If we can't keep them both, can I have one and give the other one to Mikey?"

"Mikey's mother already took one from the litter," Kelly said, avoiding the rest of the question. "Is your mom home?"

"She's in the kitchen hiding from Aunty Dorothy," the little girl replied. "Do you think David would come back if we offered *him* a puppy?"

Kelly sighed and pulled up a patio chair to sit so she could talk to Fenna without towering over her. "I don't think Dorothy really wants David back. She just didn't want him to leave."

"I don't understand," Fenna said, frowning slightly.

"Neither does Dorothy. That's the problem."

6

"Then you explain to Daddy so he can explain to us," the little girl suggested. "Daddy can explain anything to anybody. He even draws pictures."

Kelly smiled and gave a noncommittal nod. Dorothy had always looked up to her adopted older brother as well. It was true that Paul had an engineer's understanding of how things worked, but a young woman's heart wasn't as easily managed as interstellar travel.

"Hello Fenna, Ambassador," a friendly voice intoned in English.

"Uncle Dring!" Fenna exclaimed. She ran to hug the Maker who rented space in Mac's Bones for his gravity surfer, which, like the shape-shifter himself, could be reconfigured in infinite forms. "Are you staying for dinner? Mommy has been in the kitchen cooking for hours."

"Hiding from Dorothy," Kelly muttered under her breath, which drew a sad look from the Maker. "You don't know any memory wipe tricks, do you, Dring?"

"Had I not been bound to silence, I could have provided proof enough of a broken heart, even for you."

"Wait, don't tell me!" Kelly said, recognizing Jane Austen's language, but unable to place the line. It had been a while since she had played the quotation game with Dring, who was an avid reader of human literature. "Pride and Prejudice?" she hazarded a guess.

"Sense and Sensibility," he chided her.

Kelly closed her eyes for a moment and racked her brain for a quote relevant to Dorothy's state of mind. Finally, she blurted, "But what was a girl to Dombey and Son?"

Dring shook his head sympathetically. "You really are out of practice, Ambassador. Dickens, obviously."

"And the book?" Kelly demanded.

"But you already told me the book."

"I did? Oh, it's 'Dombey and Son,' isn't it?"

"Good one, Mom," Dorothy said, slouching up to the group in a shapeless garment that might have been a Verlock nightgown. "I hope you stay for dinner, Dring. Aisha makes way too much when it's her turn to cook."

"Hello, Dorothy. You haven't stopped by my garden lately. Is work keeping you that busy?"

"Work?" The fashion designer looked puzzled for a moment, as if she were trying to recall something. "What day is today?"

"Friday," Fenna piped up.

"Friday evening," Kelly appended. "If you're just getting up, you missed work again. I had a talk with Brinda just now, and everybody is worried about you at the office."

"I was tired," Dorothy said defensively. "I've been working so much lately that I needed time off to rest."

"That's not what I heard," Kelly replied, tapping her foot and waiting for a response. The mother and daughter glared at each other in a stand-off, which the Maker finally broke by changing the subject.

"Speaking of fathers and sons, I saw Joe, Paul, and Samuel head out on the Nova earlier."

"They must have gone to look at Paul's surprise anniversary present," Dorothy said.

"Paul bought Aisha something for their anniversary and he took Joe and Samuel to see it?" Kelly asked.

"No," her daughter corrected her in a bored tone. "Aisha bought Paul a bunch of abandoned space junk when Gryph auctioned it off for unpaid long-term parking bills. I guess Jeeves put her up to it."

"Here comes Daddy now," Fenna cried, pointing towards the ceiling over the small-ship parking area of Mac's Bones. The Nova was just penetrating the atmosphere retention field that kept all of the air from rushing out into Union Station's vast core when the bay doors were open. The tug set down silently thanks to a Dollnick docking system, rebuilt by Joe and Paul with help from Jeeves, which could handle small ships over short distances with manipulator fields. The Nova lowered her cargo hatch, which doubled as a ramp, and Beowulf and Samuel charged out.

"Aisha bought Paul a fleet!" the teenager yelled when he was still twenty paces away. "There are hundreds of ships in the lot. It must have cost a fortune."

"Libby?" Kelly subvoced. "Is that right?"

"I would say she got a bargain," the Stryx librarian replied privately over Kelly's implant. "Working for the Grenouthians has turned her into a tough negotiator. She also brought Jeeves to the auction with her, leading the other bidders to assume she had Stryx backing."

"What are she and Paul going to do with hundreds of alien spacecraft?"

"They haven't consulted me about their plans, but I suspect Paul and your husband will try to cannibalize enough parts to repair a number of ships in order to sell them. When owners stop keeping up with their parking fees, it's usually because they've determined the asset isn't worth the outlay."

The two men made their way to the ice harvester, stopping occasionally to retrieve Beowulf's favorite chew toy from whichever puppy ran up and dropped it in front of them, and then throwing it back towards the training area. Beowulf ignored the provocation and strode alongside Joe

9

with the air of a dog that had more important fish to fry. Samuel ran inside to report to Aisha, Fenna right behind him, and Dorothy allowed Dring to escort her up the ramp, though the Maker didn't seem to be having any success at engaging the girl in conversation.

"You should see it, Kel," Joe enthused. "Aisha finally found something to do with all that money she's been raking in." His foster son stood by quietly, looking a little dazed by his good fortune. "Go on, Paul. Get in there and thank her."

"It's not our anniversary for another three weeks," the younger man mumbled. "I haven't even gotten her anything yet."

"Just seeing your face will be all the present she needs," Kelly said with a laugh, pushing him towards the ramp. "What about you, Joe? Are you going to add a second retirement job?"

"I put some thought into that on the return trip and I've decided that it's the right time for me to step back from the training camp. I'm getting too old to teach hand-to-hand combat, and all that hardware that Aisha bought, it's like a dream come true."

"I thought you had your fill of the scrap business."

"This is different. When I took over Mac's Bones, most of the junk was really junk. I mean, it had already been picked over and crushed for recycling, and just finding a usable part was a big deal. I suppose most of the ships in the auction lot are in rough shape, but they all have intact hulls and complete systems, even if they haven't been maintained. You know that at some stage alien space technology stops advancing quickly because it becomes inefficient to constantly replace equipment that does the job just fine. We can still get parts for most of those ships, or strip them and sell the parts. Comparing Aisha's present to the old Mac's Bones inventory is like comparing a gold mine to a pile of tailings."

"If you say so," Kelly said agreeably, linking arms with her husband and strolling towards the ice harvester ramp. "As long as you're happy, I'm happy. Who do you think Thomas will bring in to replace you?"

"Probably the agent he had helping when we were on Earth. He said that she had a way with the trainees."

"The one with the sword?"

"Judith. Samuel will be happy to have somebody to practice with instead of the fencing bot."

Kelly scowled, but didn't say anything.

Two

"That green overlay must mean that they're charging their front projectors to fire. Does this ship have any defensive shields?"

"I can't figure out how to turn them on," the young man replied, desperately gesturing his way through the options presented by the holographic controller. "I hoped it would have a Stryx controller, but this ship is so old it should be in a Verlock museum. I think these are blueprints and operational procedures, but without being able to read the instructions…"

"They've fired!" the older woman said, and simultaneously, the lights on the Verlock trader dimmed to the point that the three humans could barely see each other. "You blocked it, Kevin."

"I didn't do anything," the young man protested, as power returned to the cabin lighting. "That must have been an automatic defense system. If I understand the yellow indicator up there, deflecting that attack took about a quarter of our power reserves."

"Can we outrun them?" asked the boy, who looked to be around fourteen.

"I don't think so, Nigel," Kevin said. "The Verlocks built for safety and economy. I don't think they ever cared much about speed."

"We won't be very safe if the pirates catch us again," the woman pointed out unnecessarily. "Especially after we blew up the stasis field generator and stole this ship out of their trophy yard."

"I'm sorry I got you and Nigel into this, Molly," Kevin said, looking away from the control hologram for a moment. "It was a stupid plan."

"It was a good plan," the boy insisted, keeping his eyes on the main view screen. "If the other hostages had taken ships and fled, the pirates couldn't have pursued us all."

"It's not the fault of the aliens," Molly said. "We couldn't risk telling them the plan in advance since they might have spilled the beans to our captors. Most of them are waiting to be ransomed by their families or employers."

"Two more ships are coming for us," Nigel reported, pointing at dots on the screen. "How do I control the view?"

"It's all gesture based," Kevin explained. "Just move your hands in front of the screen and try to think like a Verlock. They're very deliberate, so move slowly."

The boy began to motion with his arms, like an orchestra conductor submerged in a viscous liquid, and the view on the screen cycled through several variations. Eventually, a number of icons appeared along the bottom of the display. Nigel reached for one that looked like a ball with a tiny representation of the Verlock ship in the middle, closed his fist as if he were grabbing it, and pulled back his arm. A spherical hologram showing the space all around them sprang to life in front of the main view screen.

"That has to be us in the middle, and those three following us are pirates, but what are all of these other dots?" Nigel asked.

"I'm afraid they're more pirates," his mother replied. She started to reach towards the hologram, but a grimace of pain distorted her features, and she barely avoided crying out. "Try to zoom in. Do you see them, Kevin?"

The young man looked up from the holographic controller again, and his expression grew even grimmer. "I'll aim for the largest gap, between those four," he said, pointing at the encircling ships. "It's probably a trap, but it beats flying straight at one of them when I can't find any controls for offensive weaponry. They must have called in allied pirate crews to surround us so quickly."

The cabin lights and the hologram dimmed again, and this time the ship lurched slightly.

"We're down to fifty percent," Kevin reported. "I'm sorry, but I don't see a way out."

"I don't want to be a slave," the boy said. "I'd rather die fighting."

"Oh, Nigel." Molly regarded her son with a mixture of sadness and pride, but she knew there was nothing they could hope to accomplish against pirates in armored spacesuits.

"Hold on, this could be something," Kevin said. The controller hologram was displaying an interior view of the cabin in miniature. Situated between the acceleration chair occupied by the young man and the one shared by Nigel and his mother was a bright blue column that was pulsing with energy. "Is it a hologram of a hologram?" he asked himself out loud, making an upward gesture with his left hand. As near as he could tell, Verlocks read from bottom to top, so the previous image would be found below the current one.

"Is that a handle in the deck?" Nigel asked, leaning over to look down at the space between the two overlarge acceleration couches, which were intended for much bulkier aliens.

Kevin leaned over from his own side, the four-point restraint that couldn't pull tight to human size allowing him plenty of latitude for moving around. "Yeah. The way they show it in what I think is the instructions, I have to rotate the handle a quarter turn and then the thing will rise out of the deck." He put his words into action, wrapping his fingers around the recessed bar at the center of what looked like a circular plate, and twisting.

A glowing blue column rose up into the cabin, pulsing with light and sound. Kevin could feel the song of power throbbing in his bones, but there were no controls visible on the cylinder, and it didn't respond to hand motions.

"What is it?" Molly asked.

"It might be the thing referenced by all of the schematics I flipped through, but whether that makes it the power source or some kind of failsafe device, I don't know."

The cabin lights went out for a third time, indicating that the pirates had fired their weapons again, but the blue column seemed to be undisturbed by the energy drain.

"Maybe it's a weapon," Nigel ventured hopefully. "It looks really powerful."

"A weapon inside the cabin?" Kevin turned back to the controller and slid the hologram up and down, looking for a graphical explanation of how to activate the device and what it did. "None of this makes any sense. I think that those red squares are Verlock warning signs, but why would they show instructions at all if the thing is dangerous?"

"Maybe it's a self-destruct device," the boy said, sounding almost hopeful. "I saw a Vergallian immersive once where a crippled ship's crew took their attackers with them by exploding like a star."

"You're too young to give up," Molly told him, struggling to keep a pleading tone out of her voice. "Even if we didn't get away from the pirates this time, there will be other chances for you."

"I don't think it's a self-destruct," Kevin said. "The holograms remind me of the life boat instructions for the trader I was piloting when the pirates caught me. I think it's some kind of escape mechanism."

"Could it be a one-shot jump drive?" Molly asked. "I saw a Grenouthian documentary about faster-than-light technology a few years ago and I remember that some of the advanced species developed unique ways to fold space before they joined the Stryx tunnel network."

"Maybe it does something like that, I don't know. But I can't see how to choose a destination, much less activate it," Kevin replied.

"Who cares about where it takes us!" the boy almost shouted, pointing at the rapidly closing ships depicted in the spherical hologram. "One more shot and our defensive screens will be down. They'll match our speed, catch us with magnetic grapples, and board in armored space suits. It's how they seized our survey ship."

Kevin scrolled rapidly through holograms, looking for anything that might indicate how the cylindrical device was activated. Finally, he spotted a red box around a blue circle on the arm of an acceleration chair. He looked down and saw that a small cavity had opened just beyond where his hand would rest had he been a little larger and sitting normally. He squirmed out of half of the safety restraints and leaned forward.

"There are three buttons in the arm of my chair that might activate the device," he reported. "I didn't notice them before. The access panel must have opened when the thing rose out of the deck."

"There's one on our chair too!" Nigel confirmed. "I can barely reach all three buttons at the same time. The Verlocks must have big hands."

"Did you just press them?" his mother asked sharply.

"Nothing happened," the boy replied in disappointment.

The lights and the holograms winked out again, and this time they didn't come back on. If not for the pulsing column of blue light, the fugitives would have been sitting in the dark.

"That's it, then. We're defenseless," Kevin said. "They can fire again or come and gather us in at their leisure."

"Try your buttons," the boy urged him. "I don't care if it is a self-destruct."

The young man glanced over at the boy's mother, who gave him a sad nod, and he depressed all three of the buttons, using his pinky and ring finger together on the third one.

Nothing happened.

"I hate this!" Nigel exclaimed. "We can't fight, we can't run, we can't even see what's going on."

"Maybe you need to push the buttons together," Molly said slowly.

"I did," Kevin replied.

"Me too," her son added.

"I mean the two of you at the same time," the woman said. "It makes sense, doesn't it? It's a two-Verlock ship, and they'd want to agree before bailing out or blowing themselves up."

There was a clank on the hull as a magnetic grappler made contact. Kevin looked over at his companions, who were lit by the eerie blue glow, and said, "On three. All right?"

"Do it," the boy replied stiffly.

"One. Two. Three!"

Kevin and Nigel each pushed in their three buttons, and with a flash of blue light and a mind-bending lurch, the universe turned itself inside out. For a very long time it seemed to Kevin that his mind was floating alone in the cosmos—he tried to speak and couldn't even hear himself in his own head. He wondered if this was death, but then the main display screen flickered back on and a voice began speaking.

"You have accessed the Verlock Trading Guild's Emergency Recovery Network, better known as VTGERN."

The three humans burst out in cheers, missing a sentence of the message because they couldn't make anything of the alien script that marched up the main screen in synchronization with the audio message translated by their implants.

"...leading to the closure of this network during the reign of Shrynlenth the Two-Thousand and Seventh." The message stopped scrolling and the audio fell silent.

"What was that?" Molly cried.

"Something about the rescue network being closed," her son replied. "Can you replay it?" he asked Kevin.

"I didn't play it to start with. It just came on."

The main screen flashed again, and a different recorded message began playing back, while Verlock script scrolled up the screen in synch.

"Under the 'abandoned in place' clause of the tunnel network agreement for obsolete hyperspace infrastructure,

18

VTGERN is now under the management of a Stryx working group for transitional technologies. If you continue beyond this point, you may be charged for towing and associated rescue fees, and there will be a required payment equal to one hundred percent of the assessed value of your ship which goes to fund this working group. If you do not wish to be rerouted to the Stryx tunnel network connector, simply repeat the initiation sequence for your VTGERN device and you will be returned to your point of departure."

"What did all that mean?" Nigel asked.

"If we don't want to pay, we can go back to being captured by pirates," Kevin said with a laugh. "The Stryx can have two hundred percent of this ship as far as I'm concerned."

"Mom? Are you all right?"

Kevin looked over and saw that Molly had slumped onto her son's shoulder, her arm held at an unnatural angle.

"Don't shake her," he told Nigel. "She got banged up worse than either of us when we made our escape from that hulk. Her arm looks broken so it's better that she sleeps if she can. You've got a tough woman for a mother."

"I know that," Nigel replied, fierce pride showing in his eyes. "When Dad died, she kept right on doing the alien archeological survey work he contracted for, even though the universities offered to let her out of it."

"Rerouting to the Stryx tunnel connector," the voice announced.

A hologram appeared displaying a spiral galaxy with a large red dot accompanied by a bit of Verlock script positioned far out on one of the spiral arms. Then a network of white lines crisscrossing the galaxy leapt into existence, much denser in some areas than others. At a hundred or so well-spaced spots, the lines converged to points that looked like solid white balls due to the density of the connections.

"It's the tunnel network," Kevin said, unable to keep the awe from his voice. "I've never seen a representation like this before. The solid white balls must be the station hubs."

"We have to get Mom to a doctor." Nigel's voice sounded much younger and less certain now that the immediate danger had passed.

A blinking white line came to life connecting the red dot to one of the white balls, and a moment later, Kevin felt the familiar distortion of entering a Stryx tunnel. A weird bass rumble began rising and falling in the background, accompanied by the occasional chime.

"Maybe I better take a look at her arm," he said, slipping out of the ineffective safety restraints without bothering to undo them. "We could be in the tunnel for days."

The boy groaned with frustration and studied the hologram, trying to guess what was being depicted.

"Look, we're a quarter of the way there already!"

Kevin pivoted about and stared at the hologram. The red dot was moving up the blinking white line at an incredible clip.

"This isn't like any tunnel trip I've ever taken. I hope it doesn't scramble our brains. And I wonder what's causing all the weird sounds?"

"Maybe it's Verlock lift tube music," Nigel speculated. He stared at the moving red dot in rapt concentration, willing it to take them to their destination faster. "Why didn't we go to the nearest hub?"

"Don't know," Kevin replied. "At the speed we're moving, I guess it doesn't make much difference. We're going to be there in just a few…"

The hologram of the Milky Way disappeared, replaced by a field of stars and a giant cylindrical structure which dwarfed the arriving and departing ships to insignificance. Kevin and Nigel both found themselves closing their eyes to try to keep the cabin from spinning, which only made it worse. The ship's comm crackled to life.

"If you require assistance, do not respond to this hail and we will initiate retrieval in fifty-three seconds. Your bill for accessing the abandoned emergency network may be waived if you turn over your ship and the VTGERN device for decommissioning and can demonstrate income below the tunnel network median. Please eject any banned substances into space at this time for collection by bots. Thank you for choosing Union Station."

Kevin forced his eyes back open and stared at the hologram of the busy Stryx station in disbelief.

"Do we have any banned substances?" Nigel asked.

"We don't have anything other than the clothes on our backs. If there are drugs hidden on the ship, they can confiscate them. Whoa!" he added, tumbling back onto the acceleration couch as the ship began accelerating towards the station. "They've grabbed us with something. Hang on, Molly. I bet they have a med bot waiting in the hangar."

Three

"What happened to you?" Woojin addressed his boss. The director of EarthCent Intelligence shuffled into the meeting like a ninety-year-old man in poor health.

"Back," Clive grimaced. "I would have skipped today, but Blythe couldn't make it because she's with Chastity and the midwife waiting on the baby."

"That's right, she was almost exactly three weeks ahead of me," Lynx said, glancing at her own maternity countdown watch. "Did you try to pick her up or something?"

"The puppy," Clive replied, carefully lowering himself into a chair. He froze more than once during the process, causing the others to wince in sympathy.

"Okay, I'll bite," Walter said. "Why would you try to pick up a puppy that's almost big enough to rent out for pony-back rides? The last time I lifted any of those short-haired eating machines was to give them baths after they rolled around in—never mind."

"The kids," Clive explained. "Vivian and Jonah got the puppy to lie on a rug and they were trying to pick him up together. I had a sudden urge to show off."

"Establishing dominance," Thomas commented. "I've been told that dogs are uncomfortable in a new home until they figure out who's in charge."

"Speaking of who's in charge, why are we having this meeting?" Lynx asked.

"To discuss the upcoming review of humanity's status on the tunnel network," Clive replied. "Kelly relayed a request from the steering committee to support the ambassadors in preparing for special encounters with their alien peers. The review is taking place on every Stryx station where EarthCent has a diplomatic presence."

"How can we prepare for a Stryx review?" Thomas asked. "I'm sure they have well-defined criteria against which to measure humanity's progress, just like the test I took to establish my sentience as an artificial person. We aren't going to change their assessment now because we rush out and help alien grandmothers carry home their groceries."

Clive began to laugh and then froze again as his back went into a fresh spasm. "New rule. No making the Intelligence Director laugh."

"You should go see the Farling doctor," Woojin told him. "Look what he did for us."

"Yeah, us," Lynx groused, patting her distended abdomen and inspecting her watch again. "Twenty days, seventeen hours and thirty-two minutes until liftoff."

"I've never been much for doctors," Clive said, grimacing again. "And in answer to your question, Thomas, what the ambassadors really want is help with the confrontational part of the process, where the alien diplomats might present objections to our becoming full members of the tunnel network."

"And why did you want me here?" Walter asked.

"I assume the Galactic Free Press will be covering the review process and I was hoping that your sources might be able to shed some light on what we can expect. We haven't really concentrated any resources on trying to figure out why aliens might dislike us, though now that it comes up, I think that was probably an error on our part."

"So you expect the Grenouthians to complain that humans are cutting into their news business and the Hortens to complain that we win too many gaming tournaments?"

"I really don't know," Clive admitted. "The ambassadors have tried teasing some answers out of Stryx librarians on several stations without success, and Jeeves ignored my invitation to attend this meeting. I sent an information request to our colleagues in Drazen Intelligence asking about their own review, but it happened around a half a million years ago and their records don't go back that far."

"Does anybody really believe that the Stryx will modify their conclusions based on input from the other species?" Thomas inquired skeptically. "I'm the last sentient who is going to criticize how the Stryx go about their business, but they aren't exactly running a democracy. Clive wouldn't have pulled his back lifting that puppy if the Stryx hadn't sent Brinda to the Cayl as a hostage along with you two," he made a gesture that took in Lynx and Woojin, "while they were manipulating the emperor into preserving his empire."

"New rule," Clive groaned. "No using 'back' and 'puppy' in the same sentence. And you're probably right about the alien input being for show, but we have to make an effort to help the diplomatic branch when they put in a request. Does anybody have any ideas?"

"Go see the Farling," Woojin repeated. "He has a medical shop on the travel concourse. You'll be back to lifting puppies in no time."

Clive turned his head to give the spy agency's strategic planner the evil eye, but he froze midway as a new spasm hit.

24

"Actually, I do have one suggestion," Walter said. "I'm sure you all remember that I have a background in political science and that I dabbled a little in electoral politics when I first came to the station. In the last century before the Stryx opened Earth and, uh, deemphasized national governments, candidates for high office often staged confrontational debates."

"So you see humanity as a candidate for higher status on the tunnel network and the advanced species as debate opponents?" Lynx surmised. "That's an interesting analogy."

"I wasn't making an analogy," Walter replied impatiently. "The point is that the candidates prepared themselves for these events by staging practice debates, with advisers playing the roles of their opponents. If EarthCent Intelligence can work up a series of objections that each species is likely to raise, we could distribute a list to the ambassadors and they could practice rebutting the accusations with their staff."

"I like it," Clive said, relieved that they had come up with something that would bring the meeting closer to an end. "I'll run it by Blythe later. I mean, I'll tell her that's what we've decided."

"Maybe we could use some of the alien actors we've hired for the training camp to play the parts of the alien ambassadors for Kelly," Woojin suggested.

"Excellent idea," Walter concurred. "I've read that those practice debates worked best when staged in a manner to make them as close to the real experience as possible." He rose from his chair, touched his toes, and stretched ostentatiously. "Well, unless you need me to lift something, I've got a newspaper to run while my boss is out on maternity leave."

Nobody objected, and Walter absented himself from the meeting room. Woojin got up to make his wife a cup of decaf tea, and Thomas issued a silent command that caused a schedule for the training camp in Mac's Bones to appear on the wall-sized conference room display. The tip of one of his pinkies lit up with a laser on low intensity, and he used it to point out the organizational chart of facial images that appeared in the "staffing" section.

"What's this?" Lynx asked.

"Joe has put in for retirement," the artificial person replied. "Aisha bought Paul an alien ship graveyard for their anniversary and Joe is going to join him full-time in the salvage business."

"Does anybody have an idea how much she paid?" Woojin asked out of curiosity.

"It's public information," Clive said. "I forget the exact figure, but after Blythe got it from Libby, she commented that she knew Aisha was wealthy, but she didn't know she was that wealthy."

"Getting back to the subject at hand, Joe said that eventually he may have to kick us out of the hold to make room," Thomas informed them.

"Make room? But Mac's Bones is huge," Lynx objected.

"And Paul now owns hundreds of alien spacecraft, many of which they'll want to bring into Mac's Bones to save on commuting out to the parking orbit. Some jobs are easier in Zero-G, but for the main part, humans work better when they weigh something, not to mention having an atmosphere and other health benefits," Thomas said. "The hold won't fill up tomorrow or next cycle, but keep it in mind."

"Judith is taking his place?" Woojin asked, looking at the faces on the screen. "She's getting better with that rapier, but we don't teach fencing to the trainees and I don't remember her rating in hand-to-hand combat."

"I recently integrated a Jujitsu master upgrade from QuickU and I've been teaching her," Thomas informed them. "She'll do fine as long as she remembers that it's training and not combat. Chance is testing a Vergallian martial arts upgrade from QuickU herself, so she can always cover if Judith or I need help."

"If you can get Chance to show up in the morning," Lynx said. "Have the two of you sparred?"

Thomas gave her a sour look. "I'll just say we don't want to go to war with the Vergallians anytime soon."

"If that's everything, I'll—ohhh!" Clive groaned. "When did I become such a wimp?"

"Must be the first time you've put your back out," Woojin said sympathetically. "It's a bit of a shock, isn't it? Happened to me right before a cavalry raid, and all I did was to bend over to buckle my boots. Even loaded on pain-killers and muscle relaxants I couldn't have mounted that horse to save my life."

"Go to the beetle," Lynx told her boss. "Everybody knows you're a tough guy. You're just getting older."

"I'll walk you down there," Woojin offered. "You look like you might not make it on your own."

"I may not make it out of this chair on my own," Clive admitted. He leaned on the conference table and slowly gained his feet, though he froze like a statue more than once during the process. "Have you talked to Judith about eventually taking over so you can go back into the field?" he asked Thomas.

"Yes," the artificial person replied, moving alongside Clive, who shuffled slowly out of the EarthCent Intelligence conference room. "She said she was suspicious when you put her through the analyst training program and then never got around to assigning her a new mission after the McAllisters returned from Earth."

"It was my wife's idea," Clive said. "She believes in cross-training employees who show executive ability. Blythe also said that Judith would never make it as an analyst because she's too action-oriented, but she understands the work, and that will help her advise trainees in their career options."

"Let's go," Woojin said, guiding his boss towards a lift tube as they exited EarthCent Intelligence headquarters. "See you at home, Lynx. And I'll stop by the training camp later to discuss the changes, Thomas."

Clive braced himself for the inevitable acceleration as the lift tube capsule started off, which was a mistake since his back didn't need any encouragement to go into a fresh spasm. When they arrived on the travel concourse, he could barely bend his knees to start walking, and Woojin offered him an arm for support.

"Nuts to that," the younger man hissed through clenched teeth. "I'm not a basket case yet."

"The Farling's medical practice is just over there, between the Vergallian luggage shop and the Grenouthian entertainment boutique."

"Are you sure he's open?"

"I don't think the beetles sleep," Woojin replied. "I know he takes shifts from the Stryx as the emergency all-species doctor, and that they brought him to the station on a special contract. But he's always been here when I pop in to get Lynx her vitamins, and there's no way the Farling clock is running the same length day as ours."

"Lynx seemed pretty quiet today," Clive observed. "I know that Blythe offered to let her take the third trimester as paid leave, but your wife said that she was pregnant, not sick."

"She wouldn't know what to do with herself at home." Woojin moved quickly to interpose himself between his slowly shuffling companion and a young Horten who was obviously playing a game on a heads-up display and not watching where he was going. "Sometimes I think she would have been happier in the diplomatic branch. She enjoys the cultural attaché cover job more than intelligence work."

"Is this it?" Clive asked, eyeing the narrow entry between the luggage shop and the immersives outlet. "What's with all the stuff on the walls?"

"Sensors," Woojin explained. "The Farling scans everybody who enters his shop to cut down on diagnostic time. His bedside manner could use a little…"

"Lynx's seed donor and companion," the giant beetle greeted them, cutting off Woojin's explanation. "You've put on weight, Mr. Lynx, which you'll probably have trouble losing at your advanced age."

Woojin reflexively moved his hands to his waistline, and then jerked them away as if he had been burned. "Clive Oxford, this is Doctor M79, er, something. I've got to run." Without waiting for a response, he slipped out the door and broke into a jog, one hand on his gut.

"So, uh," Clive began, but the giant insect interrupted him.

"I see somebody has been lifting things he shouldn't," the Farling observed. "Stand over there and I'll take a blood sample. We'll have you fixed up in no time."

Clive shuffled stiffly over toward the oddly equipped operating table the doctor had indicated and extended an arm for the beetle to draw a blood sample. Instead, the

Farling pressed something that looked like a glass gun against his patient's neck. The device made a "pffft" sound, and although Clive didn't feel anything, he saw that the thin tubular section above the trigger was now full of blood. The doctor skittered over to a device that looked a bit like a vending machine, injected the gun barrel into a port, and the blood vanished from the tube.

"Alright, while that's cooking, let's see about your ruptured disc."

"Ruptured? Is that bad?"

"It would be a tragic injury if your species was carefully designed from high-grade organic structural elements, but given the crudity of your body, I think a little quick-drying glue will do the job nicely."

"Huh?"

"Up on the table, now. Don't be a baby. Oh, here," the Farling said in exasperation after watching Clive's ineffectual attempts to lever himself up. Eight insectoid appendages took hold of the intelligence director, lifting the large man and depositing him face down on the table as if he were a child.

"It's traditional for the doctor to tell the patient what he's doing," Clive gritted out.

"Really?" the Farling asked, pulling Clive's shirt out of his trousers and pushing it up to the patient's shoulder blades. "Then to put it in terms you might understand, I'm repairing your boo-boo. I could do it with you lying on your back, but then I'd have to move all of your digestive plumbing out of the way, which isn't as much fun for me as you might think. Huh. I've never seen so much vestigial fur on a human. One can easily picture you with a tail swinging through the trees."

"It's not fur, it's hair, and I'm not that bad."

"It's in the way, so off it comes," the beetle buzzed, using a specialized set of forelegs to produce the alien language translated by Clive's implant. In rapid succession, the doctor sprayed the man's back with white foam that looked like shaving cream, flashed it with an ultraviolet lamp, and then casually pulled the instantly solidified mass away and tossed it in the medical waste bin.

"What was that? I felt something."

"Just relax," the doctor continued, prodding up and down Clive's spine. "Hmm. Maybe we can avoid cutting you open after all."

"You just shaved my back and now you're not going to operate?"

"Your wife will thank me," the Farling retorted, retrieving a device that looked like an enormous stainless steel spider from an antiseptic bath. He placed it on Clive, where a number of the oddly jointed over-sized needles that looked like spider's legs immediately sank into the patient's flesh. A holographic representation of the lower part of Clive's spine sprang to life over the table, and the doctor began manipulating the spider's various surgical attachments through an embedded interface that allowed him to control the equipment telepathically.

"Did you just give me some kind of local anesthetic?" Clive asked. "I can barely feel a thing."

"Finished," the Farling declared, retrieving the spider from the man's back and casually dumping it into the disinfectant bath. "Did you want to feel pain? I'm sure I can locate a more sensitive spot to give you a jab."

"No," Clive said, gingerly rolling onto his side and then swinging his legs off the table. "Hey, I feel good!"

"Why do you say that like you're surprised? Then again, based on all of the signs of old blunt-force traumas

31

my scan picked up when you entered, I assume you've had sufficient experiences with Human medical personnel to put you off the profession."

"I spent a year as a cage-fighter when I finished my mercenary hitch. But I never broke anything so I stayed away from the docs."

"I wagered on a number of Human cage-fighting matches during my last visit to the tunnel network," the beetle commented. He watched Clive closely as the man swung his arms and twisted from side to side. "I stopped when I realized that the combatants were actually sentient, albeit in a limited way, and therefore capable of rigging the outcome. Now touch your toes."

"Come again?" Clive asked, unsure whether to be more offended by the doctor's critique of human intelligence or the aspersions cast on the integrity of cage-fighting, though he touched his toes all the same.

"That's my line to departing customers, without the interrogative at the end. Hmm. There's still something a little out of whack with your spine. I suppose it's my fault for restoring you to perfect symmetry rather than your original flawed state. Stand up straight with your back to me and push your elbows as far behind you as they'll go."

Clive followed the instructions even as he struggled to process the Farling's stream of barely veiled insults. He felt a pair of the insect's appendages hooking around his elbows and a hard, rounded surface pressed against his back. Then the doctor leaned forward, lifting Clive's feet off the ground and causing the human's body to drape over the beetle's curved carapace. A few muffled cracking sounds followed as the discs realigned, and then the alien straightened out, restoring Clive to his feet.

"Touch your toes," the doctor ordered again.

Clive shook his head at the Farling's lack of manners, but he felt so good that he complied, and this time his back moved more smoothly than it had in years.

"Another fine job," the alien complimented himself. "Will you be paying cash or should I bill your better half?"

"I'll—how much is it?"

"Shall we say, fifty creds for repairing the disc and a hundred for removing that disgusting fur?"

"Do you have a register?" Clive asked, producing his programmable cred. Whatever the alien's problem was, the director of EarthCent Intelligence didn't see the point of rising to the bait.

"It's built into the genetic analyzer to save room," the doctor said, indicating the machine into which he had earlier deposited Clive's blood. "Speaking of which, your sample should be done by now."

"Why did you need to examine my genes?" Clive asked, passing over the coin.

"Just a hobby of mine," the Farling replied absently, slipping the programmable cred into a slot and keying in the amount. "I have an interest in primitive evolutionary biology."

"Authorized," Clive confirmed for the register when the correct figure appeared floating in space. The Farling removed the coin and made a small gesture, which brought up a hologram of a colorful double-helix in the space the register display had previously occupied.

"That's odd," the Farling remarked, looking over at Clive and then back at the display. "I treated your sister earlier today."

"You must mean my sister-in-law," the man said. "My wife, Blythe, is Chastity's sister. She's expecting today, at least according to your countdown watch."

"Then she will deliver today," the doctor said confidently, "but I was talking about your younger sibling."

"I don't have any siblings," Clive said, a sudden chill running up his repaired spine. "I'm an orphan."

"As much as I hesitate to question the medical expertise of an ex-mercenary and cage-fighter, your genetic structure is too simple for there to be any mistake."

"That's impossible. I was orphaned as a child and raised by a Vergallian trader."

"Would you be willing to place a small wager on my analysis?" the Farling asked, his multifaceted eyes taking on a bright gleam.

"Whatever you like," Clive answered almost angrily. "Where is she?"

"Somewhere on the station, no doubt. I'm sure the Stryx librarian could give you her precise location. She and her son will have to return to my office two more times to complete their treatment for radiation poisoning. Shall we make it a hundred creds?"

"Done," Clive said, trying to regain the feeling of being in control for the first time since entering the alien's shop. "Libby? Can you tell me where the Farling doctor's human patients from this morning are? A woman..." he stopped and motioned for the giant beetle to continue.

"Clive's sister and nephew. Gryph is paying their bill."

"You mean the survivors from the ship that was retrieved from the obsolete Verlock rescue network," Libby responded. "I thought the boy looked familiar. I have them booked into suites in our itinerant medical hostel."

34

Four

"Another emergency meeting already," Czeros commented. "I could get used to this room."

"Watching the ships entering and leaving the core just makes me motion-sick," Kelly responded, and turned away from the transparent wall.

The elegant meeting room, reserved by the Stryx for special occasions, was built at one of the ends of the enormous cylindrical space station. It offered an outside view without the use of any imaging technology, though Kelly was unsure whether the wall was a transparent solid or an atmosphere retention field.

"Isn't that the Nova?" the Frunge ambassador continued, pointing at a tiny ship that appeared to be towing a somewhat larger craft towards the station's hollow core.

Kelly turned back, straining her eyes and her implant, but she couldn't tell whether or not it was her husband's tug because it was moving fast and was lost from view almost immediately.

"It might have been. They've been going out every day and towing in another of the alien ships from Paul's collection. I don't remember the last time I've seen Joe so excited about work."

"Ambassador," Srythlan rumbled, propelling his leathery bulk ponderously across the room. "I wish to add my personal apology to that of my government, and to official-

35

ly notify you that there is still some money left in the old compensation fund for the affected users."

"What are you talking about, Srythlan?" Kelly asked, but a flawless Vergallian beauty beat the slow-spoken Verlock ambassador to the punch.

"You must be Kelly McAllister," the Vergallian ambassador stated. "I rather expected to see you draped in jewelry, given the financial resources your family commands. I suppose you're dressed like a peasant to evoke our sympathy."

"You have the advantage of me, Ambassador...?"

"Abeva," the Vergallian responded, turning to her Horten companion. "You see, Ortha? This is what business has come to on the tunnel network. The Imperial Navy is looking for target practice vessels and authorized me to pay a reasonable price for that lot of ships the Stryx auctioned off, but the Humans stole it out from under our noses with a ridiculous cash bid. Of course, my predecessors left warnings about the favoritism shown to the newcomers by station management."

"One of our guilds sent a representative to investigate purchasing the ships to model a retro game," the Horten ambassador responded. "He turned right around and went home when that children's show host showed up with a pet Stryx in tow."

"If the two of you are referring to my daughter-in-law's purchase of scrap ships, I'd say that both of you are sore losers," Kelly retorted. "Now if you don't mind, I was talking to my Verlock colleague."

"Anybody know what this is all about?" Bork inquired, joining the knot of ambassadors. "Why isn't there any catering?"

"That's what I want to know," the Dollnick ambassador chimed in. "I got up from lunch to attend this emergency meeting, but I don't see any enemy fleets attacking the station."

"Maybe there's an assault going on at the other end," Czeros suggested helpfully.

"Ah, here's the food now," Bork declared with satisfaction. "Let's get out of the way so the caterers can do their work."

Two Gem waitresses guiding a floating catering cart cut through the clump of ambassadors and began laying the table. Jeeves floated in behind them, discussing something with the Grenouthian ambassador, who seemed to be paying more attention to the Gem than to the Stryx. The moment one of the caterers unwrapped a tray of sliced fruit, the Chert ambassador materialized out of nowhere and began transferring all of the yellow slices to his plate.

"Don't you people eat at home?" Jeeves complained, as the giant bunny he'd been attempting to converse with dodged past him in a move that was surprising for an alien who bulked nearly as much as the Verlock.

As the other ambassadors broke into a mini-stampede, Kelly hung back with Srythlan, who was both incapable of rushing anywhere, and oddly disinterested in free finger food for a diplomat. She turned to repeat her question to the Verlock, but this time Jeeves came between them.

"Thank you for coming, Ambassador Srythlan," the young Stryx addressed the Verlock formally. "May I deprive you of Ambassador McAllister's company for a moment?"

Srythlan inclined his head graciously and began shuffling towards his seat. Jeeves led Kelly back to the transparent wall with the dizzying view of ship traffic against a backdrop of the galaxy.

"What's this meeting all about, Jeeves, and why are you singling me out?"

"I'm just taking advantage of feeding time for a private word on an unrelated subject," the Stryx replied. "Are you familiar with the first contact protocols that are binding on tunnel network members?"

"I guess," Kelly replied. "But when would I ever be the first to encounter a new species? I don't go anywhere. And is there a leak on this deck? I hear running water."

"You're hearing white noise from your implant because I'm projecting an impenetrable privacy field. A word to the wise. It pays to know the protocols."

"Wait," the ambassador hissed, grabbing at and missing the Stryx's pincer as he began to move away. "Is this about the review? Will there be questions about first contact? I haven't studied for this!"

The random noise in Kelly's head cut off, and the sounds of her fellow ambassadors arguing over the remaining scraps of cross-cultural cuisine filled the room. When the last slice of citrus fruit was gone, the diplomats turned to the species-specific dishes, such as Sheezle bugs for the Dollnick, and stringy orange vegetables for the Grenouthian.

"Thanks for waiting," Kelly grumbled when she finally located the seat with 'EarthCent Ambassador' on the nameplate. "Nice job with the strategic eating."

"I saved these from Bork," Czeros said, surprising her with a small plate of crackers, a grain-based food shunned by the Frunge.

"And I rescued these from Czeros," Bork added, handing over a number of cheese slices wrapped in a napkin.

"Look who has herself a harem," Abeva commented to the table at large, bringing a guffaw from Ortha, and causing the Grenouthian ambassador to spit some masticated root vegetable into his paw to avoid inhaling it. "I can see which way the Drazens and the Frunge will be voting in the status review."

"Sentients, sentients," Srythlan said, tapping on the table to force himself to increase the tempo of his speech. "I believe that with the exception of our Grenouthian colleague and myself, this is only the second emergency meeting any of you have been called upon to attend. Since the immediate cause involves my people, the Stryx have requested that I provide a little historical context."

"We're going to be here to the end of the cycle at this rate," Czeros muttered to Kelly. "I hope they bring more food."

As if in response to the Frunge ambassador's words, another Gem appeared with a floating cart, this time a wet bar. The clone went around the table, quietly taking and filling drink orders while Srythlan droned on.

"...and so it was determined that the innovative solution we had developed produced a deleterious effect on both passengers and the fabric of the space-time continuum. Following consultation with the affected species, the Verlock Trading Guild's Emergency Recovery Network services were discontinued, and the entire project was transferred to a Stryx working group."

"Use the acronym, Srythlan," the giant bunny begged the Verlock. "We all have places to be."

"Very well," the Verlock rumbled. "VTGERN devices were recalled during the reign of Shrynlenth the Two-Thousand and Seventh, but as they were typically installed in ships without Stryx controllers, it wasn't possible to track down every last owner for notification. Recently, a ship that was lost to piracy and preserved in a private collection activated its VTGERN device and was brought to Union Station. The three humans on board are undergoing treatment for radiation poisoning, though the doctor assures me that they will all recover fully."

"That's it?" Abeva said in disgust as Srythlan settled back into his chair. "I was summoned away from an important choreography conference to discuss obsolete Verlock engineering and careless humans?"

"The view is worth the time," Crute pointed out. "I've been watching the ships coming and going and I'm proud to say that I've counted more Dollnick vessels than any other type."

"Is that including our traders?" Ortha asked skeptically.

"Naturally I excluded ships below a certain cargo capacity," the Dollnick ambassador replied.

"If you're all done with your biological activities, my elders have delegated me to address this meeting," Jeeves announced, putting an end to the casual banter. The Stryx floated to the head of the table as Czeros hastily poured himself another glass of wine and tossed it back. "Your Fillinduck colleague was unable to attend in person but is listening over a private link."

"These emergencies seem to be coming closer and closer together," the Grenouthian ambassador grumbled. "It seems like just yesterday we were meeting to discuss the breakup of the Cayl Empire, which as I recall, never took place."

Jeeves ignored the jibe and continued. "Activation of the VTGERN, while ridiculously expensive, is not the core issue. For hundreds of thousands of cycles we have been counting the rising cost of piracy and waiting for the affected species to act. The first generation Stryx agreed long ago that if the economic cost to the tunnel network exceeded a pre-determined trigger, action must be taken to change the math."

Ortha, who normally had much better control over his skin color than other adults of his species, turned bright yellow. Kelly felt a pang of sympathy for the ambassador. Everybody knew that the Hortens were over-represented in the piracy demographic, and Jeeves had just announced that the Stryx had had enough.

"What sort of action?" Bork asked in a subdued tone. Even though the Drazens and Hortens were on relatively bad terms, the idea of any species facing the wrath of the Stryx was disturbing. "Will you be suppressing piracy by force?"

"The pirate fleets are no match for even the least power-ful of the military forces of any of the established tunnel network members," Jeeves replied. "My own analysis suggests that you have come to tolerate piracy since it provides a destination for undesirables, moving the problem out of sight and mind. We're putting you on notice that if you fail to suppress organized piracy, we'll be compelled to do it for you."

The Horten ambassador inhaled sharply, perhaps the first breath he had taken since Jeeves had begun talking. Behind him, the Gem with the bartending cart tentatively raised her hand.

"Yes?" Jeeves said, pointing his pincer in her direction, which caused Ortha to change colors again as he thought the Stryx was waiting for him to provide an immediate answer.

"I couldn't help overhearing," the clone said nervously, brushing her hair back from where it had fallen over one of her eyes. "You may—I mean, I'm sure you know that during the breakdown of the Gem Empire before our revolution, a large number of my sisters fled to the pirates in search of sanctuary. Will they be given a chance to, uh, reform?"

"This is exactly why your sisters should have selected a new Ambassador after Gwendolyn returned home," Jeeves scolded her. "My recommendation is that you get together and choose somebody to represent you on Union Station so you can participate in the process."

"We were saving the spot for Gwendolyn to return," the Gem protested. "Besides, my sisters have had a bad experience with government."

"What about her question, Jeeves?" Kelly asked. "Have you already judged the pirates in absentia?"

"We haven't done anything other than to tally up the costs," Jeeves replied in exasperation. "The first generation Stryx, and myself for that matter, expect you to discuss this rationally amongst yourselves, come up with a plan of action, and contact your respective governments for the necessary resources. In fact, I suspect that my continued presence may only disrupt your negotiations, so I will leave now."

Several of the ambassadors spoke at once in an attempt to get more information from the Stryx, but he put his words into action so quickly that there was a popping sound as the air rushed in to fill the space he had occupied a moment earlier.

"Do you have another bottle of this excellent vintage?" Czeros asked the Gem, apparently unperturbed by the turn of events.

"I could use a refill myself," Ortha said, turning around in his seat to address the clone. "Same as I had before, but double the Urpo. No, on second thought, triple it."

"Maybe we should be inviting her to sit rather than ordering drinks," Kelly suggested.

"Drinks first, sit second," Czeros stated. "Do you realize what the Stryx are demanding of us, Ambassador McAllister?"

"They want us to agree on a plan to do something about the pirates," Kelly replied. "It seems reasonable enough, and as Jeeves said, they can hardly be a match for any of your fleets."

"Seeing how this crisis was precipitated by the actions of Humans, I trust we can count on you to take the central role?" Abeva inquired sweetly.

"Well, EarthCent doesn't actually have a fleet," Kelly said apologetically. "We don't really have any warships at all when it comes right down to it."

"Perhaps it's time you bought a few," Crute suggested. "I'm sure I could arrange to provide surplus Dollnick hardware at rock-bottom prices with attractive financing."

"Be reasonable," Czeros said. "It makes no sense for Humans to spend money on a navy while their only useful world is a Stryx protectorate."

"I supposed that's true," Abeva acknowledged graciously. "Even if they had warships, they'd likely just get in our way, or lose them to the pirates and exacerbate the problem. But surely we can expect EarthCent to shoulder its fair share by offsetting a portion of the expenses for the rest of us."

"Second the motion," the Grenouthian ambassador said quickly.

"Third," Ortha rasped, after downing his triple strength drink.

"All in favor?" Abeva proposed.

"Wait a minute," Kelly interrupted. "We haven't even decided on how to proceed yet. What point is there to voting on Earth's financial participation when my authority barely extends to the local embassy budget? Even there, my office manager gets angry if I spend down the petty cash without consulting her first."

"Ambassadors, calm yourselves," Srythlan pleaded. "The Stryx have been delaying action for over a hundred thousand cycles. Surely we can get through a brief meeting without finger pointing and punitive votes."

"That from the species that created VTGERN," the Chert ambassador muttered. Then he seemed to realize that he had spoken loudly enough for the Verlock to hear, triggered his shoulder-mounted invisibility projector, and disappeared.

"So we've been drafted onto a new committee," Bork concluded in a tired voice. "Somebody has to take point, and I think that Ortha..."

"Why does everybody always blame us for the pirates?" the Horten demanded, his anger fueled by the triple Urpo. "You heard the Gem. The clones have probably been the fastest growing segment of the pirate population in recent years."

"I'm only a bartender," the Gem protested, backing away from the table. She pressed a button that slid the covers into place over the levitating bar cart and began pushing it towards the exit. "I just remembered that I have to be at another job."

"Good going, Ortha," Czeros grunted. "If that's it for drink service, I see no reason to extend this meeting any

44

longer than necessary. The question of what to do about the pirates is not going to be resolved today, and determining how it will be accomplished is a job for military and intelligence specialists."

"I understand that EarthCent Intelligence is headquartered on this station," Abeva said with a condescending smile. "That makes them naturals for the job."

"If you want the Humans telling you how to deploy the Imperial fleet, I have no objection," the Frunge ambassador replied.

"Why are you all in such a hurry to deploy military resources?" Ortha demanded. "Perhaps if we spoke to the pirates, we could convince them to change their ways." After looking around the table to see how his suggestion had been received, the Horten ambassador amended himself. "Forget I said that. I'm not usually a heavy drinker."

"I believe we must act, and quickly," the Grenouthian ambassador said. "If we don't do something to change the second derivative of the piracy function, the Stryx might choose to zero it out. I will instruct my staff to search for precedents that may indicate how far we must bend the curve to prevent heavy-handed intervention."

"I will do the same," Srythlan declared, and the other ambassadors made various noises of assent, falling in line behind the representatives of the two oldest and most powerful species on the tunnel network.

"What's he talking about?" Kelly whispered to Bork.

"We need to determine the degree to which we must suppress piracy to meet the Stryx demands."

"Does the EarthCent ambassador have a thought to share with us?" Abeva inquired, raising one perfectly shaped eyebrow.

"Well, yes," Kelly rose to the bait. "If I understand our Grenouthian colleague, it sounds like you want to determine a sustainable level for piracy rather than stamping it out."

"Pretty bloody-minded for a species without a single warship," Crute observed.

"Everything in moderation," Srythlan rumbled.

"Perhaps our Horten colleague could open a channel of communication with the pirates," the Grenouthian ambassador suggested. "I'm sure that the rest of us need to consult with our governments before committing to any course of action, and as my esteemed Frunge colleague has pointed out, there's no point in sitting around here just for the view."

"My schedule is booked solid through the next cycle," Crute complained. "I vote we schedule a follow-up meeting right now so the Stryx don't drag us out of prior commitments again."

"Second the motion," the Chert ambassador spoke out of thin air.

"Third," Abeva said. "I'm surprised Ambassador McAllister hasn't offered to host the meeting. According to the briefing I received from my predecessor, she volunteers as a matter of course."

Kelly bit back her immediate reaction, having learned that speaking up at multi-species meetings was a good way to get stuck in charge.

"Motion is carried," the Dollnick ambassador declared reluctantly. "I request that my previous and the following statement in no way be construed as a commitment on my part to assume official chairmanship of this committee, a position which I suggest we decide at a meeting point two-zero cycles from today in my embassy. If anybody objects to the timing, you're welcome to reschedule at your own embassy."

Nobody spoke up. In fact, the more fleet-footed ambassadors basically fled the room.

"A word, Ambassador McAllister," Kelly heard in a bass rumble as the remaining diplomats rose to exit the room. She turned and saw that Srythlan had remained in his seat. "I would like to continue our previous discussion," the Verlock ambassador added, and by the time he reached the last word, the room had cleared.

"Of course, Srythlan. Was there something I can do to help?"

"The Verlock Trader's Guild established a compensation fund for purchasers of the VTGERN device when the system was discontinued. My legal advisers inform me that as probationary members of the tunnel network, Humans qualify to file claims for medical expenses and suffering caused by using VTGERN. There is also a refund for the purchase of the device, but that amount goes directly to the Stryx working group, which I understand has taken possession in exchange for waiving the cost of the rescue."

"That's very nice of you to offer, Srythlan. It turns out that two of the people involved are related to the Oxfords, and I understand from Blythe that the medical treatments are going well and the Stryx are picking up the tab."

"In that case, the medical compensation money will be paid to the victims in cash," the Verlock said. "The rules of the fund are quite clear."

"I'll let them know," Kelly offered. "By the way, can you explain why the Grenouthian ambassador seemed so sympathetic to the pirates?"

"Grenouthian ships are far too advanced to be troubled by the freebooters, and more importantly, their news networks rely on a certain level of piracy for content. I suspect that pirates play a role in not a few Grenouthian entertainment products as well."

"The bunnies get financial backing from the pirates?" Kelly asked in astonishment.

"I meant that pirates frequently appear as characters in dramas," Srythlan explained. "I am not a fan of immersive productions myself, but I have sat through a number of premiers from various species in my professional capacity. To the extent that I was able to follow the overwrought action, it appeared to me that most of them relied heavily on piracy to advance the plot."

Five

"Metoo," Kelly greeted the young Stryx. "Thank you for coming. Go right in. Everybody else is already here."

"You're not participating?"

"Jeeves said that I would probably go all wobbly and try to stick up for Dorothy. I think he's right, so I'm going to leave and hide in the embassy."

Metoo dipped in acknowledgement and then floated up the ramp into the ice harvester. Jeeves was waiting just inside the door, and the two Stryx engaged in a silent conversation that was over in less than a pico-second. Shaina and Brinda were sitting at the table in the dining area, along with Affie, Flazint, Chance and Blythe. Beowulf stood watch over the two puppies who were sprawled on the rug in front of the couch, fast asleep after a busy morning of mischief.

"Where is she?" Metoo asked when he reached the table.

"In the bathroom," Blythe replied. "Kelly says that she spends half of her life in there now."

"It's really that bad?" Metoo gave a metallic shudder. "I had hoped that Jeeves was exaggerating."

"Look at this," the older Stryx commanded, opening a garment bag and removing what looked like a large black sack draped with crepe. "She was supposed to be working

49

on a new line of vacation frocks and this is what she brought in as a prototype."

"Maybe she was thinking about combining vacations with funerals," Metoo suggested, in defense of his childhood friend. "Humans have limited time and budgets compared to the other species, and I've observed that they often mix business with pleasure when they travel."

"It's called an expense account," Blythe explained, and then raised a finger to her lips and whispered, "Shhh. Here she comes."

"Don't even start on me, Mom," Dorothy declared combatively as she walked into the room, her eyes so downcast that she didn't even notice the visitors. "I worked late yesterday so I'm just going to lie down on the couch for a bit."

"Hi, Dorothy," Jeeves said, causing the girl to spin around and trip over one of the sleeping puppies.

"Did I forget a meeting?" Dorothy asked, rubbing her eyes and surveying the group. "Metoo! What are you doing back on Union Station?"

"Jeeves invited me. He said you haven't been yourself lately."

"I haven't been—Blythe! You too?"

"We're your friends, Dorothy. Chastity wanted to be here as well, but Marcus got freaked out about the idea of her going out with a six-day-old infant, or even worse, leaving him to babysit."

"What is this?" Dorothy asked, trying to back away and finding herself blocked by Beowulf, who had moved into position behind her. Her eyes went wide when the reality hit her, and she practically shrieked, "Are you staging an intervention?"

"You're depressed, Dorothy," Shaina told her firmly. "You're sleeping all of the time, you're not eating and losing weight, and you aren't paying attention to work."

"I'm just taking a little break, is all. Am I supposed to be a slave to SBJ Fashions?"

"You haven't come out dancing since David left," Chance said, not hesitating to use the taboo name. "You don't get any exercise, and Samuel tells me that you haven't worn high heels in three months."

"I get exercise. I played fetch with the puppies just yesterday."

"I was at the training camp and I watched you," the artificial person retorted. "You came down the ramp with a rubber bone, threw it, and then went back inside and closed the door while the puppies ran to get it. You were just getting rid of them, and I had to assign Judith to chase them around the hold for an hour so they wouldn't interrupt our drills."

"Look at this...thing," Flazint said, indicating the black garment Jeeves had brought along. "Would you really want to see your worst enemy wearing it?"

"It's not so bad," Dorothy protested. "Black is elegant."

"I bet Flazint that I could wear it out to a club and still get free drink offers," Affie said. "I lost. The bartenders at two places even asked me to leave because I was hurting business."

"Well, it's good to have clothes to let people know that you're sad. We can't all be happy and perky all the time."

"Dorothy, we miss you at work," Brinda said. "The shoe prototypes haven't progressed one bit since you broke up..."

"I don't care about shoes anymore. I'm going back to bed," Dorothy declared, but the giant dog refused to let her pass. "Et tu, Beowulf?"

"Dorothy," spoke a gentle old voice, and the girl froze in place. "Look at me. I want to talk with you." The ambassador's daughter turned reluctantly back to the group and was confronted by a hologram of her grandmother.

"No fair," Dorothy muttered, staring daggers at Jeeves.

"Kelly has told me all about it and you're behaving like a little girl," the hologram of Marge continued. "You didn't want to marry the boy, and now you think you have the right to make everybody else miserable because he was smart enough to marry somebody else? From what I understand, you practically pushed the two of them together."

"Why is everybody ganging up on me?" Dorothy cried, and sinking to the floor, she wrapped her arms around one of the sleeping puppies and began to sob.

"That's a good girl, let it all out," her grandmother cooed. "You're not even twenty-two yet and you have your whole life ahead of you. Just think about all the people who love you and want you to be happy."

"But I found him in the lost-and-found and bought him pizza!" Dorothy wailed. "He was mine."

"Maybe you were just holding him until his real owner came along to claim him," Metoo suggested.

Flazint and Affie exchanged looks, taken back by the display of histrionics, the likes of which they had thought only existed in Earth's unpopular immersive dramas. Chance went over to Dorothy and began patting her on the back.

"That's better," Marge said. "I have something on the stove so I need to go now. Thank you, Jeeves." The hologram winked out, and the remaining participants in the intervention looked at each other, uncertain of what to do next.

"I've got to get going too," Blythe said. "I'm taking Clive's sister and her boy out to dinner. You'll meet them at Paul and Aisha's anniversary party."

"Metoo and I have to be, uh, somewhere," Jeeves said, sounding uncharacteristically subdued. The two Stryx fled the ice harvester as fast as they could without creating sonic booms.

The Hadad sisters talked quietly with Affie and Flazint while Dorothy bathed the still-sleeping puppy in tears. Eventually, Brinda snuck into the kitchen and made a pot of tea.

"Is this sort of thing normal with you guys when practice relationships don't work out?" Affie whispered to the sister who remained.

Shaina rolled her eyes. "Not so much at her age, but she was pretty young when they started dating, so I guess we can cut her some slack."

"I have a hedge friend whose older sister's engagement fell through after twenty years of negotiations," Flazint whispered. "She didn't mist herself for months and her hair vines got all dried out."

"I always felt a bit guilty about the whole pheromone control business, but if it saves me from this..." Affie commented.

Beowulf suddenly stood up and gave a puzzled bark. The puppies came awake in response, and the one who Dorothy had been using as a furry handkerchief rose to his feet and shook himself off, spraying salty tears around him.

"Ugh," the artificial person and girl chorused together, and then Dorothy laughed for the first time in months.

Somebody rapped on the hollow sheet metal of the open hatch with his knuckles, and then a tall young man with rust-colored hair stuck his head into the ice harvester. "Is anybody home?"

Beowulf bounded up to the man and went into a paroxysm of sniffing and tail-wagging. The puppies likewise took an instant liking to the stranger, competing at jumping up and putting their paws on his shoulders, and taking turns licking his face.

"Whoa, boys," the young man protested. "I didn't think I'd ever see a bigger dog than Beowulf, but I guess Mr. McAllister found one."

"Kevin?" Dorothy asked, rubbing her swollen eyes in disbelief. "Kevin Crick?"

"You remember me," Kevin said in relief. "I didn't think you would after fifteen years. You look terrific."

"I do?" Dorothy said, shooting a look over at the Hadad sisters, both of whom winked and flashed a thumbs-up sign. "I mean, I just got up. Give me a second to—oh, what am I wearing!"

The girl fled the room, and Kevin stood in the doorway looking uncertain about what to do next. Chance went over and grabbed his arm to make sure he remained.

"Sit down. We were just having tea, or at least, they were," the artificial person said, turning on the charm. "I'm Chance, and I'm one of Dorothy's best friends. These four are Flazint, Affie, Shaina and Brinda. How do you know Dorothy and Beowulf?"

"My family camped in the hold to repair our ship when I was seven, and then we went on a vacation to Kasil together."

54

"That's where I recognize the name from," Shaina declared. "Brinda and I ran the auction with Jeeves. I remember it was your sister who had the visions that brought the whole thing about."

"Becky," Kevin confirmed. "She ended up going to New Kasil and starting some sort of a religious commune. Most of my family lives there now, but I became an independent trader. Is all of Dorothy's family still, uh…"

"Alive?" Chance completed the sentence for him. "Yes. Joe and Paul are out sorting through a mess of alien spacecraft that Paul's wife bought him, Kelly is at work, and Samuel is either at school or dance practice, though you probably never met him if I'm doing the math right. Beowulf obviously remembers you, and the puppies are his."

"I remember Beowulf, but he was older and fatter than this dog," Kevin replied doubtfully.

"Oh, he was reincarnated," Brinda explained. "Beowulf came back as a full-blooded Cayl hound, and I have the only other one on the station, at least until they got together and had the puppies. Do you want one? They seem to like you."

"Uh, sure, if they're okay with Zero G. Not that I have a ship anymore."

"What happened to it?"

"Pirates," Kevin gave the one-word answer. "I escaped with a woman and her son who turned out to be related to some people here on the station."

"You're the guy who showed up with Clive's sister?" Shaina asked. "But everybody is talking about that. If it wasn't for the Farling doctor, Clive and his sister never would have known that the other one even existed."

"Yeah, her family is really nice. That Clive guy even offered me a job and help setting up as a trader again, though I guess I'm not supposed to talk about that."

"You must mean as an EarthCent Intelligence agent," the Frunge girl guessed. "It's okay, everybody on the station knows about it. The secret training camp is a few steps from here, and Chance is one of the instructors."

"I teach people how to interact with aliens and extract information in social situations," the artificial person said proudly. "My guy, Thomas, runs the camp now that Joe is retired."

Kevin looked from one woman to the next in a sort of a daze, overloaded by the information dump covering everything from canine life-after-death to alien relations.

"What have you guys been doing to Kevin?" Dorothy demanded, approaching the table. She was now wearing one of the SBJ Fashions tube dresses that she had helped design, high heels, and had somehow found the time to apply enough makeup to partially disguise the fact that her eyes were swollen from crying. "Not telling tales, I hope."

"I was just getting him caught up on your family," Chance replied. "It turns out that Kevin's the guy who escaped the pirates with the sister Clive didn't know he had."

"He agreed to take a puppy when he gets settled," Brinda added.

"That's great," Dorothy said, not really listening to the explanations since all of her attention was focused on Kevin. "Are you hungry? I'm famished, and there's a ton of stuff in the kitchen. Hang on a sec." Not waiting for a reply, she disappeared again, and Shaina got up to go help.

"She looks different than five minutes ago," Kevin commented, unaware of exactly how much of a transformation had taken place. "I guess she must have been up late."

"Did you like her dress?" Affie asked. "She designed that one, though I helped with the colors and Flazint did the zipper."

"It looked fantastic," the young man replied, running worryingly low on his store of adjectives. "She works as a fashion designer?"

"For SBJ Fashions," Brinda confirmed. That's 'S' for my sister Shaina, 'B' for me, and 'J' for Jeeves, but he's not here."

"I remember Jeeves," Kevin said. "He hung around with Paul. And Dorothy had a Stryx friend from school, Metoo. Is he still around?"

"You just missed him, but he's rarely on Union Station these days."

"Try my mom's lasagna," Dorothy said, placing a tray with two heaping plates of food on the table. "Don't worry about the others. Shaina is bringing out some sliced fruit for Flazint and Affie, and she and Brinda ate before coming."

"How about Miss, uh, Chance?"

"She's an artificial person," Dorothy replied, and then began to shovel food into her mouth like she hadn't eaten in three months.

Kevin couldn't help noticing that the women were eyeing him speculatively, and he tried to cover his embarrassment by beginning to eat, even though he had just come from a late breakfast. The young man had spent a reasonable amount of time around Frunge and Vergallians as an independent trader, and it seemed to him that the two aliens, along with the artificial person and the two older women, were sizing him up for something.

"So, how have you been?" he asked between bites, bringing some smothered snorts from the others.

"Pretty good," Dorothy lied smoothly. "Well, I broke up with my boyfriend a few months ago, but it was no big deal. He eloped with a woman that my mom brought back from Earth to live with us. Do you want to see our office later? We could always use a man's opinion."

Affie rolled her eyes at Flazint, more in reaction to the idea that a male could have anything useful to say about women's fashion than as a commentary on their friend's sudden transformation.

"He eloped with a woman who was staying in your home?" Kevin asked, stopping with a fork halfway between the plate and his mouth. "Sounds like a real jerk."

"Oh no, he's a great guy," Dorothy insisted. "Hannah was pretty nice too, and she was really good at sewing. I think they made a perfect couple."

"He couldn't dance to save his life, though," Chance commented.

"David put up with a lot," Flazint added, then clamped her hand over her mouth.

Beowulf thumped his tail at the mention of David's name, and then dropped his head over Kevin's shoulder from behind, staring down at the lasagna.

"He must have been crazy to run out on you," Kevin declared loyally, causing Dorothy to blush lightly, but it only showed on her neck, where she hadn't applied the Horten cosmetic spray.

"I guess we just had different expectations," Dorothy said, as if she were thinking about it rationally for the first time. "He wanted to get married right away, open a little

58

restaurant somewhere, and have a big family. I still want to see new places and discover new inspirations for fashion. He had a really hard childhood and had to run away from a job where they didn't care if he lived or died, so I kind of get now why settling down was so important to him."

"Shaina and I have to get going," Brinda announced, rising from the table. "You kids have fun, and we'll see you in work tomorrow, Dorothy."

"Tell Jeeves to burn that weird black dress," Dorothy called after them. "I don't know what he was thinking."

"Are you interested in Clive's offer?" Chance asked the young man. "There's a new group of trainees starting in a couple of weeks and it would be no problem to fit you in."

"Oh, do," Dorothy said, putting her hand on Kevin's arm. "It'll be fun. You can have dinner with us every night and get to know the puppies."

"Maybe he doesn't want to be a spy," Affie said, reading Kevin's face. "He doesn't look like an organizational man to me."

"I bet I can get you work with my Dad and Paul," Dorothy rushed on. "My sister-in-law just bought them a huge lot of alien ships at an auction and they need help just figuring out what they have."

"Ships?" Kevin repeated, his mind seizing on the word. "I think Chance mentioned that earlier. I lost my ship to the pirates, and the Stryx took the old Verlock trader we arrived in as a payment for rescuing us."

"I can get you a ship," Dorothy promised impulsively. "We have lots of them."

"I'm not looking for a free lunch," Kevin protested. Then he looked down at the remains of the lasagna and had to laugh at himself. He set the plate on the floor for Beowulf, who warned off the puppies with a deep growl before demolishing the leftovers with a single swipe of his tongue. "I'd love to talk to your father and brother about work, and if they can't use me, I'll think about Clive's offer. I've been taking care of myself since I was sixteen, and from what I remember of this place, there must be plenty of opportunities."

"Where are you staying?"

"The station manager put us in a quarantine suite after our first radiation poisoning treatment," Kevin explained. "We can go out and mix with people now, but it's a free place to stay until the monitoring period is over. Everybody is being really nice about it, like it was their fault that we stole an obsolete Verlock ship out of a pirate's museum and accessed a discontinued rescue network."

"We should really get back to work too," Flazint said, nudging Affie. "It was nice to meet you, Kevin."

"We really hope you stay around," Affie added.

"Well, if all of you are leaving, I guess I'll go check and see if I'm needed on the training grounds," Chance announced. "I think I may be late."

"Where are you going?" Dorothy cried, as Kevin scraped back his chair.

"I just thought that if everybody else was going…"

"No, you stay. Or better yet, why don't I show you around the station. Have you been to Libbyland?"

"Never even heard of it," Kevin admitted.

"Great. Libby lets us in for free in return for feedback. Let me get my purse, I'll just be a minute. Maybe five, this dress is wrong for Libbyland. Play with the puppies."

Kevin found himself alone with the dogs while Dorothy disappeared again. Beowulf brought him a throwing toy that looked like a boomerang, barked for the puppies to come, and then led the group down the ramp. Kevin cocked his arm, aimed for the far side of the hold, and cast the toy.

Too late the young man and the dogs realized that the giant bay doors were open. The throwing toy shot through the atmosphere retention field and disappeared into the vacuum of the station's core as the Nova began dropping into the hold, a two-man Sharf trader towed in tandem with a rigid cable.

The puppies set up a howling that attracted the attention of the recruits all the way over in the training area, but Beowulf just gave Kevin a sad look before trotting out to meet the Nova.

"What happened?" Dorothy asked, coming down the ramp in a casual skirt and sandals.

"I threw their boomerang into space by mistake," he said, marveling at how the girl's height seemed to go up and down as if by magic.

"Don't worry, they have too many toys. Let's get going," she added, grabbing his wrist and tugging him towards the exit. "There's lots of neat stuff to see. You can talk to Dad and Paul when we come back for dinner."

Six

"I'd like to start with a Drazen if it's not too much trouble," Kelly requested. She felt bad about interrupting the alien encounters training session, but Thomas had assured her that the agreement EarthCent Intelligence had struck with the various alien theatrical guilds left them chronically oversupplied with actors.

"One Drazen, coming up," Judith replied brightly. "Hey, Lorth. Front and center."

A middle-aged Drazen who was dressed like a lounge lizard detached himself from the collection of otherwise unoccupied aliens who were trading war stories about their work in the immersives. He sauntered over to the two human women and gave Kelly an appraising look.

"Will I be acting as her escort?" Lorth inquired, giving the ambassador a friendly leer. "I've had some experience in that line of work when money was tight."

"What? No. I need you to play the part of the Drazen ambassador, Bork. He's a friend, but it wouldn't have been right for me to ask him to do something like this."

"Like what?"

"Humanity is up for review on our tunnel network membership status. We're hoping to get off of probation. Part of the process is that our ambassadors on the Stryx stations are meeting with their alien counterparts to hear any feedback they might have. Our analysts have drawn up a list of issues they believe are relevant for each species and I'd like to practice my responses."

"That sounds a bit like overkill," the actor replied, absently pulling on an earlobe with his tentacle. "Why would you want to get off of probationary status, anyway?"

"I'm not quite sure myself," Kelly admitted. "I don't have access to the information that would explain it."

"It's your funeral," Lorth observed with a shrug. He gave Judith the thumbs-up and guided the ambassador to one the designated areas where alien actors and human trainees did their pair work. "Can you zap the script to my implant so I can read it off my heads-up display?"

"It's just a few questions for improvisation. I have them right here." Kelly fished in her purse and handed the actor a thin sheet of plastic.

Lorth studied the script for just a second before he broke out laughing. He looked away out of politeness, lest the ambassador think that he was laughing in her face, but every time he turned back, he set off in fresh gales. Kelly couldn't help finding it a little disconcerting, and she peeked at his sheet to make sure it was the correct one.

Eventually, the actor regained his composure, and said, "I hope these questions weren't drawn up by any of the agents I've helped train or I'm doing a very poor job indeed."

"What do you mean?" Kelly asked. "What's wrong with them?"

"All of these complaints imply that we see you as competition," Lorth replied, and then hastily added, "No offense."

"None taken. But don't the Drazen independent traders and market vendors complain about humans undercutting prices with shoddy merchandise?"

"Sure, but they say the same sorts of things about all of the species. It's just natural. I know I can get better quality knives from the Frunge at a good price, or the latest high-tech gadgets from the Dollnicks, not to mention more interesting dramas from the Hortens and the Vergallians. But in the end, I mainly buy from Drazens because they understand me, and if I ever get a part, I expect them to make up the majority of the audience."

"But isn't the whole idea of the tunnel network to bring us all closer together?" the ambassador followed up.

"Yes and no," the under-employed actor replied. "I'm sure you're aware that the Stryx stations are unique places. You'll find relatively few imported manufactured goods on any of the developed worlds, mainly specialized equipment, collectibles, and odd food-stuffs. I understand that the excellent hot sauce I put on my grizzards is produced on your homeworld and exported by Drazen Foods, but how much of my diet does it really make up? A thousandth of my daily calories? Less?"

"Hmm, I see your point. So if you were the Drazen ambassador and you were meeting with me to complain about humanity, what sorts of things would you bring up?"

Lorth stopped looking directly into Kelly's eyes and shifted his gaze to a spot above her head, as if he were checking for a tentacle. "I really couldn't say," he mumbled.

"Come on," Kelly urged him. "I'm sure there's something about humans that gets under your skin. How long have you been helping with the training improvisations for EarthCent Intelligence?"

"Around eight cycles total," the Drazen admitted. "It's steady money between real gigs. But the closest I've ever come to diplomacy was playing chauffeur for an emissary in a historical drama. I'd really rather not mislead you with my personal views."

"Very well," Kelly replied with a sigh. "Could you ask if there's a Frunge available to talk with me?"

Lorth nodded in the affirmative and excused himself, his body language expressing obvious relief as he fled back to the other actors. Kelly frowned and flipped through the scripts in her purse, looking for the questions the intelligence analysts had drawn up for a Frunge. After reading the English translations under each line, she used her stylus to rub out the ones related to human competition in the edged weapons and cutlery trades.

"Hi, I'm Yzmith," a mature Frunge woman introduced herself.

"Kelly McAllister," the ambassador said. "Did Lorth explain the role to you?"

"Yes, I'm looking forward to giving it a try," Yzmith said with a smile.

"Here are the questions for improvisation," Kelly told her, handing over the plastic sheet and crossing her fingers. The Frunge glanced at the text and began to shake with silent laughter, her hair vines rustling up a storm.

"What? I got rid of the ones about us competing with your metallurgists."

"You think we're offended by your grain eating?" Yzmith asked with barely restrained mirth. "Look, I wouldn't get caught dead ordering one of your pizzas with crust because the neighbors would shun me if they saw it delivered. But abstaining from eating grass-related foods is just a fetish with Frunge diplomats and some of the old families who take legends seriously. I mean, I don't believe that the grasses on our homeworld were ever sentient, so

65

how could they have agreed to a treaty? It's just one of those things, like Verlocks sacrificing virgins to appease the volcano gods."

"The Verlocks sacrifice virgins?" Kelly asked in horror.

"Not anymore, I don't think," Yzmith said. "I just meant it's a cultural identity thing that some of us take more seriously than others." She lowered her voice and looked around before adding, "I recently installed hardwood flooring in my bedroom because it's much nicer than walking around on a metal deck, even with rugs. It's not like the lumber came from my ancestors."

"I see." The ambassador made a mental note to have Dorothy check with Flazint on whether the woman was exaggerating. "Are there any problems with living around humans that you would bring up if you were a Frunge diplomat?"

"Well, you do keep funny hours, and your deck lighting tilts a bit too far towards the red end of the spectrum, but it's better than the heat lamps some other species need to see properly."

"Lighting," Kelly said. "I'm not sure we can really do anything about that. Isn't there something else?"

"Nooo," Yzmith replied, looking a bit antsy. "But I may not be typical. Do you want me to send in a different Frunge?"

"I think I saw a Horten, so if he's not engaged, I'd like to see if the questions we worked up for him are relevant."

"I'll send him right over," the Frunge woman said, walking away as quickly as dignity and manners allowed.

Kelly pulled out the Horten questions, hesitated with her stylus, and then decided to leave them unaltered. A minute later, a surly-looking alien approached her.

"I'm Kelly McAllister," the ambassador introduced herself.

"Thunta," the Horten replied shortly. "I'm not so sure about this."

"Sure how? If you feel uncomfortable about changing colors, I can look away."

"Why would I care what a Human thought of my appearance?" the actor responded dismissively. "The point is, I don't believe that impersonating a Horten diplomat for the amusement of the EarthCent ambassador is covered by our contract. I would have taken it to the steward, but he's busy over there hamming it up in the role of a customs agent. If you ask me, he missed his calling as a petty government official."

"Perhaps if you look at the script?" Kelly prompted, passing over the questions. The Horten glanced down at the plastic sheet and turned a deep brown, his breathing becoming ragged as he struggled to contain himself. Then he couldn't take it anymore and he broke out in short, sharp shouts of glee, drawing the attention of the role-playing pairs working around them.

Judith hurried over and asked, "Is there a problem?"

"He's just expressing his opinion about the questions I wanted him to ask," Kelly explained. "It seems possible that our intelligence analysts missed the boat on this exercise. I'll just ask him if he has any suggestions of his own, provided that he's willing. I'm afraid he feels that the contract doesn't cover this contingency."

"No, please, I can do this," Thunta declared, pulling himself together. "I've always considered myself to be more of a dramatic actor than a comedian, but it's a chance to stretch some unused theatrical muscles. Let's see." The Horten's skin tone returned to a neutral beige, and he

67

struck a pose that was eerily reminiscent of how Ambassador Ortha appeared when he was feeling self-important. "How do you account for the unprecedented success of Humans at recent Horten gaming tournaments?" the actor inquired, and then his skin shifted back to brown and he fell on the floor snorting.

"I don't see what's so funny," Kelly protested. "I don't claim to follow the gaming news myself, but I understand that humans have been taking home the bulk of the prize money at some Horten tournaments."

Thunta struggled to control himself, failed, and then crouching and facing away from Kelly, extended an arm back over his shoulder brandishing the questions.

"Here, take them," the Horten begged. "It's too much. I thought I could do it, but it's just too funny. I don't know how comic actors manage."

Kelly snatched back the plastic sheet and wasted a sour expression on the alien's back. "Are you going to explain your reaction?"

"You think that we're angry about Humans winning at our tournaments? Your wins are in games where our players have allowed their skills to deteriorate due to the lack of competition. Everybody knows that both attendance at tournaments and remote viewership are up at least three-fold since your players went on their streak and gave our people a rooting interest again. The scores and the times that Humans have been posting wouldn't have gotten them into the finals a few thousand years ago, but the level of play has deteriorated that badly. I'm not even a fan, but I can appreciate the value of opponents one can loathe."

"Loathe?" Kelly didn't know whether to be pleased with the back-handed compliment or to worry about the underlying sentiment. "Uh, thank you for your input." She motioned to Judith, who had been keeping an eye on them since the Horten's noisy collapse.

"He's not typical, even for a Horten," Judith whispered as she stepped around the ambassador to help the actor to his feet.

"Do you have a Dollnick?" Kelly asked, half hoping that the answer would be negative.

"Sure. He's one of our best role players and he's just finishing up with a demonstration of how to comport oneself in the presence of a merchant prince. I'll send him over in a minute."

Kelly easily found the Dollnick script among the remaining sheets, since the number had been decreasing as she folded the used ones in half before replacing them in her purse. She scanned the questions and wasn't surprised to see that they concentrated on business-related issues, which she was now convinced would simply tickle the alien's funny bone.

"Libby?" she subvoced.

"Yes, Ambassador," the station librarian responded over her implant.

"I was just practicing for the review confrontations, but the alien actors keep laughing at the questions we prepared. I know you aren't going to tell me what to expect in the review, but I'm making a fool out of myself here."

"Better with the actors than with the ambassadors," Libby replied philosophically.

"Just a little hint?" Kelly pleaded.

"How many Vergallians are there?"

"What? Uh, I think around a trillion, right? They have hundreds of worlds, after all."

"And how about the Verlocks?

"Not as many, I think. Maybe a half a trillion?"

"And the Drazens, and the Hortens, and the Frunge?"

"I think they're all in the same ballpark," Kelly hazarded a guess. "Haven't we been through this before? You're implying that the alien species all outnumber us by so much that we don't rate on any sort of threat scale."

"I was just asking you questions," Libby replied innocently. "I believe your Dollnick is waiting."

Kelly brought her eyes down to humanoid level and found herself staring at the chest of a giant Dollnick. She tilted her head back to peer up at the alien's face, and introduced herself. "I'm Kelly McAllister, the EarthCent Ambassador."

"Glure," the Dollnick trilled in reply. "I understand there are some jokes for me to read."

"Questions, about issues your people may have with humanity," Kelly corrected him, handing over the plastic sheet. "Don't hurt yourself trying to suppress it if you feel the need to laugh."

"I'm a professional," Glure replied haughtily, accepting the sheet with one of his bottom arms. He glanced at the list, and immediately startled Kelly by giving a loud clap using his upper set of arms. She looked up again and saw that the Dollnick's face was swelling in an alarming manner, as if he was holding his breath. Then he mastered his physical reaction and cleared his throat with a series of untranslatable whistles.

"Are you ready?" Kelly asked.

"So I go first?" Glure responded. "I thought you would start the dialogue in such a way that I would be required to use one of these lines in a naturalistic manner. All right then. Why do Human workers who have signed long-term contracts organize themselves into non-familial groupings and try to demand changes to the working conditions, compensation, etc." Here the Dollnick clapped again, and let out a long burst of chirps and tweets.

"What's so funny about that?" the ambassador asked in frustration.

"I'm just an actor, not a grammarian, but I've spent enough time working here to identify certain phrases that carry a different connotation in Dollnick than in your native tongue. My understanding of the question I just read is that workers who have signed an iron-clad contract sometimes put themselves to a great deal of trouble and aggravation in hopes of changing the terms with no chance of achieving their aims. How is that not funny?"

"But surely the aggravation is shared."

"No, I don't see that it is," Glure replied seriously. "Nobody could terraform worlds or conduct interstellar trade if contracts were subject to reinterpretation on the part of unsatisfied parties. Let me give you an example. If I came in today and told Thomas that I wanted a raise in the negotiated rate I'm being paid under the contract, I'm sure he would find it amusing rather than upsetting."

"I'm not sure I agree, but how about the other questions?"

"Variations on a theme. Whoever composed this list appears to believe that Dollnicks are bothered by Humans getting themselves worked up and complaining about this or that." He shook his head. "What other species do you have left? Maybe you'll get lucky with a different set of questions."

"Vergallian," Kelly replied with a grimace.

"I think our Vergallian got a real part last week because I haven't seen her since," Glure replied. "I'll ask Judith."

Kelly felt deflated as she folded the script returned by the Dollnick and pulled out the only remaining unused sheet. She read over the English translations beneath the Vergallian script and shook her head.

A tall young man approached the ambassador, a light fencing foil carried in his right hand. "Hi, Mom. Judith said you needed a Vergallian role player, and I'm the closest thing available today."

"When did you start working for the training camp?"

"It's a barter deal, in return for unlimited time with the fencing bot. I'm supposed to ask you some questions?"

Kelly felt exceedingly awkward, but she didn't want to embarrass her son by sending him away, so she handed over the sheet. "Here. You can just read the English."

"What's the point of that?" Samuel asked. "The translations don't actually match the Vergallian that closely, you know."

"Wait. You read Vergallian now?"

"Sure, Libby taught me. When I start at the Open University, I'm going to combine Vergallian Studies with Space Engineering."

"When did all of this happen? I thought you were barely keeping up with your lessons and spending all of your time dancing and watching Vergallian dramas!"

"Libby gave me credit in cultural immersion training for all of that. And I'm going to start working a few shifts at the station lost-and-found to pay for school."

Kelly stared at her son in shock. How could he have grown up so suddenly without her noticing? "Hold on a second. Are you taller than me now?"

"I've been taller than you for months, Mom," Samuel replied in a pitying voice. "Anyway, these questions are kind of silly in English, but in Vergallian, they're hilarious.

Why don't you explain to me what you want and I'll rewrite them."

"I appreciate the offer, Samuel, but EarthCent Intelligence came up with the list based on an analysis of our economic and political interactions with the other tunnel network species," Kelly explained patiently. "The idea was to prepare me for any objections the aliens might raise to our becoming full tunnel network members."

"But they don't care about any of this stuff," the fifteen-year-old objected. "The Vergallians have a saying, 'Better the smelly, uncouth servant that you know than a rogue robot,' which is why they're always willing to hire humans. Besides, if I learned one thing being on 'Let's Make Friends' for two years, it's that the other species all accept that the Stryx are going to do what they think is best in the end, regardless of any voting."

"That may be true, but I'm sure you can understand why I, and the other ambassadors, want to put our best foot forward," Kelly said.

"So when you have your meetings, listen to what the alien ambassadors say, and pretend you understand what they mean. I learned that on Aisha's show, too."

Seven

Paul manipulated the field of view for the Nova's main screen and asked, "What do you think of this one?"

"Looks like a small support vessel of some sort that got turned inside-out," Joe replied. "I've never seen a ship anything like that, so it could just as easily be a colony transport for ant-sized aliens, or a tunnel hog for remote control asteroid mining."

"Can't you ask the station librarian?" Kevin suggested from the jump seat on the rear bulkhead of the tug's bridge.

"I queried Libby, but she gave me the old 'competitive information' excuse," Paul replied. "Do you think it could be two small ships that drifted into each other and got tangled up?"

Joe shook his head. "I can't imagine that Gryph would allow anything like that to happen, even if the former owners did stop paying their parking fees. With all of those outriggers and mechanical linkages it could be almost anything. That bit on the end looks like a giant pair of scissors."

Paul nodded. "I think you're right, but it's weird to imagine that any species advanced enough to reach a Stryx station would be holding onto rocks with claw attachments and making holes with twist drills. I guess we better take a closer look before we try hauling it back."

"That's why we have spacesuits," Joe said happily. He knew that Paul was in a hurry to get a handle on the hundreds of abandoned ships that Aisha had won at the auction, but some things just took time. The ex-mercenary savored the opportunity to go exploring a mere twenty-minute commute from Mac's Bones, and he felt like he was entering a second childhood.

"We have a spare suit that would fit you in the locker, Kevin, but it would be a big help if you could watch the bridge and release the tow cable if we need to place it manually," Paul said.

"As long as Beowulf promises to keep the puppies in line," the young man replied, moving up and settling into the pilot's seat.

The dog opened one eye on hearing his name, managed a skeptical look, and then went back to sleep. Although he was a pure-bred Cayl hound by way of the Huravian monks, the original Beowulf's dislike of Zero-G had made the transfer through his reincarnation, albeit diluted. The puppies had no such issues with weightlessness, and by employing a combination of dog-paddling through the air and bouncing off everything in sight, they followed Joe and Paul to the lower deck.

"When was the last time you suited up?" Joe asked over the helmet comm, after the two men were encased in their spacesuits.

"Must be over a year ago, when we were helping out the circus troupe that bought a lemon of a transport from some con artist who set up a dealership in Earth orbit. They were lucky that their oxygen didn't run out in the tunnel. First time I've ever seen a Sharf hull that couldn't hold an atmosphere. The dealer must have bought it out of a salvage yard."

"I can't remember the last time I used the evacuation lock," Joe said, pushing gently off the bulkhead next to the suit locker and drifting slowly towards the emergency exit. "It would be a lot simpler to just open the main hatch and float out through the atmosphere retention field, but the puppies might try to follow us."

"Beat you there," Paul challenged him, kicking off harder than the older man and zipping past him towards the round access door with the heavy plate of glass in the center. He hit the large green button next to the evacuation lock as he landed, and the door slid to the side, revealing a short tube that could accommodate a single space-suited humanoid. "See you outside."

Joe arrived just as the door slid shut, and he watched through the small window as Paul launched himself out of the tube and the suit's maneuvering system began to steer him towards the strange alien craft that they had observed on the Nova's main viewer. The outer hatch closed automatically, and then it was Joe's turn to hit the green button. This time there was a loud hiss as the atmosphere from the ship rushed to fill the vacuum, but it was a small space, and it only took a moment for the pressure to equalize before the door slid fully open.

Two minutes later, the men reached their destination at about the same time, thanks to Joe overriding his suit's maneuvering system, which was programmed to make the most efficient use of limited fuel. From up close, the ship looked even weirder than it had on the view screen. Some of the various arms and crane-like mechanical contrivances might have been intended for asteroid prospecting, but one of the longest pieces looked remarkably like a conveyer belt, which made no sense in Zero-G.

"Do you think this thing was capable of atmospheric reentry?" Paul asked. "I can't see it happening, unless the ship can project some kind of force field as an envelope."

"Doesn't make sense. Any species capable of manipulating energy like that wouldn't be using a conveyer to move material. I'm slipping around the back side for a look."

"I'll check out that bit that looks like a mounting bracket to see if it's solid enough for a rigid tow cable."

The two men used the manual controls on their suits to head off in different directions, and almost immediately, Joe let out a low whistle.

"It's got treads! This thing isn't a spacecraft at all. I'd say it's a high-end wrecker or service platform. If we can get it working then it will really come in handy in Mac's Bones. I still feel bad about selling off all the old heavy equipment when we got out of the junk business."

"Sounds good to me. I'm looking at this bracket, and going by the thickness of the alloy, it must be tied into the bones pretty well."

"Think you can snake the tow cable over from the Nova without getting caught up on all the gear? We could have Kevin release it and just place the grapnel manually."

"I could guide that tow cable through here with one eye closed," Paul boasted. "Besides, it has to be a straight path or the cable could be damaged when we turn on the juice and it goes rigid. Beat you back to the Nova."

Joe was on the wrong side of the wrecker when Paul issued the second challenge and jetted off, so he satisfied himself with muttering, "Cheater," and letting the suit maneuvering system plot the return on default settings. As the suit brought him around the undercarriage of the alien contraption, the light-beam from his chest-mounted suit lamp played over a boxy-looking structure with what appeared to be large, rectangular viewports, floating not far away. "I see something interesting that must not mass enough to have made it past your filter algo," he reported to Paul. "It might be a candidate for the thing that Jeeves suggested."

"Is this a trick to slow me down, or do you really have something?"

"It's not a ship in any normal sense of the word," Joe observed as he drew closer to the alien construct. "I'd guess it was a temporary habitat of some sort, maybe for a construction crew laying a keel. Wait. I see some large portal on this side that reminds me of the stackers that the Sharf put on some of their big container carriers."

"I'm homing on your location," Paul replied. "Sounds like it could work out perfectly."

Joe continued his slow inspection of the small habitat from a safe distance, manually manipulating his suit light to examine the find. "I haven't spotted any damage yet. The question is whether it has the structural integrity to stand up to gravity."

"It's angular acceleration, not gravity," Paul corrected him over the suit comm.

"As long as there's an up and a down and my feet don't float off the floor, a giant centrifuge like Union Station is gravity enough for me."

"Right behind you," the younger man announced as his suit brought him to a halt alongside Joe. He toggled his own chest-mounted light to high intensity and joined the survey. "I think it has potential. Is it all open space inside? There's enough height for two or three decks, assuming that bit there is the base."

"I thought I'd let you have the first look inside since it belongs to you."

Paul goosed the maneuvering system to bring the suit alongside one of the large viewports and played his light around the interior. "Empty, but I can see a door and partitions, and it's built on humanoid scale."

"We'll have to get moving on this right away if you want it to be ready in time for the party."

"Did you see anything we could use as a tow point?"

"No, but it's a good chance to try out your new salvage net."

"We can't bring it back to Mac's Bones," Paul said. "I want it to be a surprise."

"I already talked to Brool at the Dollnick small ship facility and told him we might bring something in. I've sent them a lot of business over the years, and besides, they're more likely than we are to have tools that can cut whatever this stuff is without shredding it."

"I'm more worried about whether it will hold paint. These outer bulkheads are pretty pristine for having been exposed to space for however long."

"Gryph shields the whole area. Besides, it's not a bad color."

"I think it's the exact same shade of green as the bathroom walls in the Empire Convention Center," Paul retorted. "Jeeves says it keeps most species from wanting to stay in there any longer than they have to, which translates into less space wasted on facilities. Come on. Let's get back and deploy the net. If I have to pay the Dollys to do most of the work, I will."

"I'm not racing," Joe informed his foster son as the younger man did a neat flip and shot off towards the Nova. The ex-mercenary again left his own suit-maneuvering system on the default settings and took his time looking around on the trip back.

79

"Uh, we might have a bit of a problem," Paul reported over the helmet comm from where he was floating by the evacuation lock. "Looks like one of the puppies figured out how to open the inner door and worked his way into the tube. He's lucky he didn't open the outer hatch by mistake or he'd be a goner."

"Where's Kevin?"

"All I can see is—aw, he's licking the viewport. Good thing the hull hasn't had time to radiate off its heat load or his tongue would freeze on there."

"Nova," Joe commanded over his suit comm. "Voice patch with confirmation."

"Voice patch enabled," the controller replied.

"Nova. Disable control pad in evacuation lock until further notice."

"Pad disabled."

"I should have thought of that," Paul said, then began tapping the viewport with one gauntleted finger. "Bad dog," he mouthed through the transparent faceplate of the helmet. The puppy gave a toothy smile and licked the viewport again.

"Nova, enable ship paging."

"Paging enabled."

"Kevin. One of the puppies has gotten into the evacuation lock. I've disabled the controls so he can't vent himself into the vacuum, but you're going to have to get him out."

"Can you hear me?" Kevin's voice replied, sounding like he was talking from a distance with his head in an enclosed space.

"We hear you," Joe responded.

"I've got a bit of a situation with the other puppy," the young man said. "He figured out how to open the door to one of the lockers and got tangled up in some kind of netting."

"Oh, no," Paul groaned. "He must have triggered the firing mechanism that spreads the net over the target. Now we're going to have to drag it into place with our suits."

"Hey, I just realized something," Joe said. "With both of the puppies bottled up, we can just drop the main hatch and float in through the atmosphere retention field. Be with you in a minute, Kevin."

"Do you have any idea how big that net is?" Paul grumbled over the helmet comm. The two men employed the manual maneuvering jets on their suits to work their way around the stern to the main hatch. "Jeeves said it would be illegal to use it in space if he wasn't a Stryx."

"He's just bragging. Nova, confirm atmosphere retention field integrity."

"Field strength optimal."

"Nova, open main hatch."

The top of the large hatch that doubled as a cargo ramp slowly moved away from the ship in an arc, and as soon as there was enough clearance to enter, both of the space-walkers grabbed the lip and propelled themselves into the tug. They quickly removed their helmets, but left the suits on.

"What a mess," Paul exclaimed, finding nearly the entire hold was filled with loose folds of the heavy monofilament netting. "How can one puppy cause so much trouble?"

"I've been trying to get him free without having to do any cutting, but he's not exactly cooperating," Kevin said. "Is the net valuable?"

"I'm not sure. Jeeves gave it to me, and I doubt you can cut it with anything we have on the ship."

"I think I'm tangled up worse than the puppy now," Kevin admitted. "I've got to say that he's been pretty calm about the whole thing."

"Speaking of which, I should get the other puppy out of the evacuation lock before he develops claustrophobia," Joe said. "I think that would be easier if you activated your magnetic cleats," he added for Kevin's benefit.

"I'm not wearing them," the young man replied dolefully. "Dorothy wanted me to try on these Horten-style boots to give her feedback. She says she has an idea about a footwear line for traders."

"I'll get you a pair of the old buckle-ons," Paul offered, activating his own cleats and then shuffling along the deck towards a storage locker. Like Joe, he'd had enough of floating around in Zero-G for one day. "You know, the mesh should be big enough to let both you and the puppy through. It just looks solid because you've got a net big enough to hold a spaceship deployed in a small space."

"I wondered about that. So if I just start pulling the mesh over both of us, eventually we'll put the whole mess behind us."

"Yeah, but do it facing the bulkhead," Paul cautioned him. "I can see from here that the main part of the net is between us. The puppy must have been caught near the edge when he triggered it."

"You should have heard him howl," Kevin said, pulling a large pentagonal section of mesh over himself and the puppy.

"Incoming," Joe called, pulling the second puppy out of the evacuation lock, and then pushing him gently towards the ladder to the bridge. "Go see Beowulf."

The floating puppy barely cleared the edge of the billowing net, and to everybody's relief, he hooked the ladder with a paw, and then carefully made his way through the opening to the bridge and disappeared.

"I think we're out," Kevin said. "At least, there's no netting between us and the bulkhead."

"I'm coming with the cleats," Paul responded, and cautiously began making his way past the billowing net. "I wonder why it seems to want to fill up the whole space rather than bunching."

"Could be some sort of static charge," Joe speculated. "It doesn't look like it's attracted to the metal as much as it's repulsing itself, and I guess it stayed away from the main hatch because of the atmosphere retention field at this end. What did Jeeves say it's made of?"

"Some kind of crystalline monofilament, but he had it done up special by a Verlock lab on the station. He said it works on a principle similar to our tow cable, except instead of the crystals aligning and going rigid when it's powered up, the current will increase the strength of the net by several orders of magnitude. Just hold onto the puppy and stick your feet out, Kevin. I'll strap the cleats on for you."

"Thanks. I'm sorry I didn't keep a better eye on them."

"Wasn't your job," Joe said. "We let them follow us down here. I'll have to reset all of the control pads so that a warm paw won't open any locks."

Kevin kept one arm around the giant puppy while he ran the other between the bulkhead and the netting and made his way to the ladder. The tendency of the net to expand into all of the space available meant that he had to stop several times to get it clear of his feet, which he slid forward on the magnetic cleats rather than lifting them off the deck. Eventually he was able to send the puppy after its brother up the passage to the bridge.

"Feel up to a space walk to net a habitat?" Paul asked Kevin.

"I've got a better idea," Joe cut in. "What do you think would happen if we crept the Nova up to the target, sealed the bridge, and then dropped the ramp?"

"You mean you'd blow the air out of the hold and let it take the net with it?" Paul looked at the tangled folds of mesh speculatively. "Can you aim it?"

"I won't miss," Joe said confidently. "We used to practice decompression net casting as a way to discourage boarders when my unit served a stint on a Vergallian ship doing anti-piracy patrols. Even though armored spacesuits can make short work of a light net, nobody likes to see one coming at them. I'll drop the ramp all the way down and then cut the atmosphere retention field so it blows out all at one. All of the air in the hold doesn't mass enough for the exhaust to throw us into anything."

"Should we try to untangle the net first?" Kevin asked.

"I'm hoping the static repulsion does that for us," Joe replied. "Worst thing that can happen is that you and Paul will have to suit up and chase it down to drag into place by hand. I've had enough floating around for one day. Let's make sure all of the lockers are sealed and that there's nothing unsecured down here."

After confirming that the only loose item in the hold was the giant net, the three men joined the dogs on the upper deck and Paul closed the rarely used hatch at the top of the ladder as a double precaution. Even though the bridge had its own atmosphere retention field, it hadn't been tested with explosive decompression of the hold.

"Switching to visual," Paul announced. He changed the display from the enhanced sensor mode that created

84

images from a blend of radar and infrared to the visible light spectrum. "I'm going to inch her over on manual."

Firing the navigation thrusters on short pulses, the pilot expertly maneuvered the Nova to a position about ten ship lengths from the small habitat. Then he pulled his hands out of the holo-controller and said, "Your turn."

"Nova. Bring us around to, uh, seventy degrees on axis," Joe commanded. The ship controller fired a couple of small thrusters that imparted a slow axial spin to the ship, bringing the main hatch around to face the boxy habitat. "Close enough. Nova. Drop technical deck atmosphere retention field."

"The main hatch is open," the controller warned him.

"Nova. Override safety protocols," Joe instructed.

There was a gentle lurch as the atmosphere blew out of the hatch, taking with it the net, which expanded gracefully to its full extent just before it touched the habitat, where momentum drove the edges forward to wrap the target in a large mesh bag.

"Target secured," Paul reported. "Let's hook the pull-cord and go see a Dollnick about a paint job."

Eight

"Who invited the Farling?" Herl inquired, not bothering to lower his voice.

"If it isn't the head of Drazen Intelligence," the giant bug replied. "It makes one wonder what the tail of Drazen Intelligence might look like."

"I invited him," Clive interjected, stepping between the two aliens. "He's my doctor."

"He's my doctor too, when I'm on the station, but that doesn't mean I'd ever invite him to a poker game," Herl replied. "Didn't it occur to you that a creature who can diagnose the ills of another species is likely to be an expert in reading body language? The Farlings are so sensitive to heat and moisture that they can tell if most biologicals are lying from across the room. On top of everything else, he counts cards!"

"A sore loser with a long memory," the Farling commented, rearranging a couple of chairs so he could lean forward on the sectioned front of his belly armor, the closest his carapace allowed him to come to sitting. "Have you regained full use of your tentacle?"

"It's fine now," Herl allowed grudgingly, taking his seat as far from the doctor as possible. "I stopped doing the stretching exercises after I returned to Drazen Prime and my personal physician told me they were no longer necessary."

"The exercises were never necessary," the Farling informed him. "I just found it amusing to think of you faithfully doing them."

"You really invited him just because he's your doctor?" the Drazen spy asked again, turning back to the director of EarthCent Intelligence.

"Well, that and I lost a bet," Clive admitted. "He agreed to let me off the hook if I could find him some new suckers."

"And based on who I see coming, your debt is cancelled," the Farling declared.

"What's he doing here?" Woojin asked, pulling out a chair.

"Clive lost a bet," Herl replied sourly. "No Lynx tonight?"

"She's at her baby shower, just a couple of weeks to go."

"I read about those in our backgrounder on Human culture. Aren't they usually held a little earlier?"

"Showers are an old tradition, from the days when people thought pregnant women shouldn't leave the house, and nobody was quite sure when the baby would actually arrive. But Doc here gave her a countdown watch and a guarantee."

"You're welcome," the Farling said. "Will this evening be an all-male game?"

"Yes. We're expecting two more, but Daniel's wife is hosting the shower and Walter is helping him set up," Clive replied. "They're married to sisters."

"The more the merrier," the insect doctor buzzed. "Unless it includes those two," he added in a subdued fashion, indicating the approaching pair with a leg.

"Hello, M793qK," Jeeves rattled off. "Taking time away from your busy business for a little recreational gambling?"

"Not if I knew ahead of time that you'd be here," the Farling retorted. "Hello, Dring."

"I assure you that neither the young Stryx nor myself employ unfair advantages when playing cards with the younger species," the Maker replied. "I assume we can count on you to do the same."

The giant beetle unfolded his wings from his carapace as if he were considering flying off, then tucked them back in again. "I suppose I can make an exception in your honor, Dring."

"Here we go," Joe said, pushing his homemade bar cart over to the table. "I finally got around to mounting a keg so nobody will have to run back and forth to fill pitchers. Can I interest you in a beer, Doc?"

"I shall make the attempt in order to be sociable," the Farling responded.

"Great. I asked Paul to mix up a couple of Divverflips before he headed out, Herl." Joe put on heavy rubber gloves, unscrewed the lid of a ceramic-lined thermos, and poured out a toxic beverage for the Drazen. "Nothing for Jeeves, beer for the rest," he continued, drawing glass after glass of his home-brew.

"Did Kelly already leave for the shower?" Clive asked. "I've got a few new items to pass along."

"She actually went into the embassy a couple of hours ago to prepare for the status review, despite the fact she doesn't have a clue what to expect," Joe said. "All I could get out of her is that she's memorizing first contact protocols like she expects a pop quiz. I'm sure the ladies will ping her if she doesn't show up on time."

"Are you referring to a review of humanity's status on the Stryx tunnel network?" the doctor inquired. "I didn't realize you were sufficiently advanced to be considered for full membership."

"And as the Farlings never saw fit to join the tunnel network, this concerns you how?" Jeeves retorted.

"I might be persuaded to place a small wager..."

"How much?" several voices asked at once.

"I see you weren't exaggerating the action," the Farling said, turning his head in Clive's direction. "I wouldn't want to make any of you uncomfortable, so how about twenty creds each, just to keep it interesting. Of course, I must exclude our Stryx friend from the offer as I'm sure he already knows the results."

"Which outcome are you betting on?" Woojin demanded.

"You have to ask?

"I'll go twenty," Joe said. "It would be disloyal to Kelly not to."

"If you put it that way, I'll back the EarthCent Ambassador as well," Dring concurred.

"I guess it comes with my job," Clive added, nodding to the Farling.

"Herl?" the insect inquired.

"Stranger things have happened," the Drazen mumbled, nodding his assent.

"Don't tell Lynx," Woojin said, accepting the bet. "Ever since her morning sickness stopped on the day that Doc predicted, she thinks he's infallible."

"You really are biologically simple creatures, even for humanoids," the Farling said, flexing his mandibles good humouredly. "So how does this game work?"

"You've never played poker?" Joe asked, breaking into a broad grin.

"Clive said that there are cards and chips involved, so I'm sure I'll pick it right up. I brought my own deck if you want to try a Farling game."

"That won't be necessary," Herl said hastily. "Give me the cards, Joe, and I'll run him through the hands while you cash us in."

The owner of Mac's Bones slid a box of cards across the table to the Drazen, and then began accepting creds from the players in return for chips.

"A simple game of valuing hands based on magnitude, suits, progressions, and collections of like cards," the Farling commented as the Drazen Intelligence head rushed through examples. "That will be sufficient as I'm sure I can infer the rest from the pattern. How much may I change into chips?"

"This is a friendly game," Joe explained. "The yellows are ten millicreds, the reds are a hundred, and the blues are one cred. Most of the players buy in with twenty creds."

"Then change me twenty creds," the Farling said, producing a coin seemingly out of thin air.

Herl groaned. "I forgot to mention that he does sleight-of-hand tricks."

"I believe it's my turn to deal first," Dring said, holding out a hand with stubby fingers for the deck. "Seven-card stud will offer our new player a good overview of betting while reinforcing the rankings of the cards."

"Stud? As in a breeding male? A piece of jewelry for a body piercing? A construction member?"

"Stud poker refers to games where most of the cards are dealt face-up," Jeeves explained to the Farling. "Dring's

90

preferred version of seven-card stud starts with an ante, followed by two face-down cards and one face-up. The best hand showing controls the bet, with suit deciding ties."

"There are hundreds of versions," Joe added. "Some of them originated in different regions on Earth, some I think the guys in the mercenaries just made up on the spot. So, what do you think of the beer, Doc?"

"It has an interesting visual appearance," the Farling replied, studying the glass through multi-faceted eyes. "The aroma is quite muted for a Human beverage, and the carbonation appears to be natural." Grasping the mug with the same set of specialized legs he used for rubbing out audible communications, the giant insect raised the beer and tipped it back so the contents poured into his mouth. After replacing the empty mug on the table, the Farling rubbed out, "Not bad," while simultaneously burping.

"Show off," Herl muttered, and took a hit from his Divverflip.

"Allow me," Joe said, reaching over for the mug and refilling it from the cart-mounted keg.

"Ante is two yellows, gentlemen," Dring announced, starting off the pot with a pair of his own chips. Then he began shooting cards around the table, not pausing until he placed a face-up card on his own pair of down cards. "And the king bets."

"Another twenty," Herl said, pushing in the chips.

"Not very confident in that king, are you?" the Farling inquired.

"He just wants to keep us in," Woojin said, but paid the price anyway.

91

"Dealer plays," Dring declared, adding another two chips.

Joe turned his two of diamonds over to go with his concealed five of clubs and eight of hearts. "Fold."

"Are three spades a good start?" the Farling asked.

"It depends what you're starting," Herl replied. "Of course, asking doesn't mean you have them."

"Of course. I shall buy another to see what happens."

"I'll double it again," Jeeves said, putting in a red chip and taking back four yellows. "Not that I have anything to write the Galactic Free Press about, but I wanted you to know that raising the bet is always an option," he added for his neighbor's benefit.

"And it's not worth sixty for me to see the next card," Clive said, folding.

The others all cast suspicious looks at Jeeves, but they paid up, and Dring dealt the second open card.

"Lady Luck favors our newcomer," the Maker remarked. "Ace of spades bets."

"You said the ace was at the bottom of the rankings," the Farling accused Herl.

"Only for low straights and only in some games," Joe told him. The Drazen simply looked amused and took another sip from his drink.

"Then my ace will bet a hundred," the doctor said, pushing a red chip into the pot.

Jeeves contributed a red chip of his own without comment, and Herl pushed in a hundred, looking unhappy about it. Woojin snuck another look at his hole cards, grimaced, and mucked his hand, followed by Dring.

"I'm more intimidating than I realized," the Farling declared. "You know, I think a little salt would match well with this beverage."

"Right here," Joe said, taking a bag of pretzels from the cart, opening it, and filling a bowl while Dring dealt the remaining three players another up-card. The sound of furniture being knocked over and claws scratching at metal decking immediately followed, and before Herl received his next card, two hopeful looking puppies and one very large hound arrived at the table.

"Do they play poker?" the beetle asked, eying the dogs speculatively.

"Beowulf used to sit in for me when I went on beer runs, but he'd rather just eat pretzels," Joe replied, flipping three snacks into the air like a spread of torpedoes to ensure that each of the mooches could get one.

Dring completed the deal and announced, "Pair of aces bets."

"Perhaps a blue," the Farling said, sliding the chip forward, and then using the same limb to extract a pretzel from the bowl. "Is the substrate of this salt delivery system edible?"

Jeeves folded, and Herl absently gnawed the tip of his tentacle for a moment before conceding the pot with a growl.

"It's just flour and water," Joe replied.

The Farling transferred the pretzel to his mandibles and gave an experimental nibble while raking in the pot. "I believe the wheat flour has been adulterated with niacin, reduced iron, and folic acid. Hmm, on second taste, add thiamine mononitrate and riboflavin to the list. The flour has been further mixed with malt, dextrose, some type of unidentifiable vegetable oil, soda, and the remains of millions of single-celled fungi."

"If the dogs knew Farling they'd be gagging right now," Woojin said.

"Naw, Beowulf knows all about yeast," Joe pointed out. "Can't brew beer without it."

"Five card draw," Woojin declared, gathering the cards and shuffling. "Same ante, nothing wild, no drawing four on an ace."

"Is it normally allowed to change the value of an ace by drawing on it?" the Farling asked. "It seems like you would require a new deck every hand."

"Draw poker allows you to replace cards that don't help you by drawing new cards from the dealer," Clive explained. "You can ask for up to three cards, but some games allow you to draw four cards on an ace. There's a betting round after the cards are dealt, and another after the draw. The dealer can also call a blind, a forced bet to get things started, but we rarely play that."

Woojin completed the deal rapidly and the players all studied their cards. Joe, Woojin, and Clive held their hands mercenary style, up close to their chests, while Dring held his cupped between both hands. Herl quickly rearranged his cards and then returned them to the table. The Farling, whose head was already low due to his belly-down position, barely raised the top edge of his cards and surveyed them on the table. Jeeves let out his version of a snort.

"Worried that I'm going to sneak a peek, M793qK?"

"While I accept Dring's statement that neither of you would knowingly take advantage at cards, it's been my experience that young Stryx are the nosiest sentients in creation," the Farling replied. "Busybodies, as well."

"A hundred," Dring announced, tossing a red chip in the pot.

"You guys showing off for the Doc or something?" Joe grumbled, moving in a red chip of his own.

"Is it me already?" The Farling toyed with his blue stack and then tossed a single red into the center of the table. "I hear that for your latest performance, Jeeves, you've decided to tinker in the age-old business of freebooting."

"Fold," the Stryx said. "Are you upset because the pirates handle distribution for the Farling-manufactured illicit drugs in this part of the galaxy?"

Clive looked up sharply, folding his hand as an afterthought. "The pirates are part of the drug trade? I thought they only operated on the boundaries of the tunnel network."

"Call," Herl said, flipping in a red chip. "Pirate ships stay on the fringes of civilized space, but their crime syndicates reach into the holdings of many tunnel network members."

Woojin pushed a red chip into the pot and picked up the deck. "How many?"

"I'll take two," Dring said, dropping his discards and picking up the two replacements dealt by his neighbor.

"Three," Joe announced, looking sadly at the Maker, who almost never bluffed. "My unit used to work some anti-piracy operations for the Vergallians. You said, 'many,' Herl. Which species are immune?"

"None for me," the Farling said, eliciting a groan from the Drazen. "Crime doesn't create criminals, it attracts them. The Verlocks have little tolerance for such behavior, but the Grenouthians have always been a bit shady."

"One," Herl spat, throwing out a card and glaring at the giant insect. "Your analysis of our characters only extends to the two oldest oxygen breathing species on the tunnel network?"

"Dealer takes three," Woojin announced, making up his hand. "Your bet, Dring."

"Pass," the Maker said.

"I suppose it's time to find out what effect these blue chips have," the Farling mused. "I'll put in five, one for each card of my flush. And as to my analysis of tunnel network members, Herl, species come and species go. I'm waiting to see if the rest of you stick."

"You're bluffing," the Drazen Intelligence chief barked, his tentacle standing rigid behind his head. He reached for his blue chips, hesitated, looked at his cards again, and folded. "It's not you I'm afraid of, but anything beats a missed straight."

"I'm on a strict allowance," Woojin said, tossing in his own hand.

"Are you aware that a full house beats a flush, M793qK?" Dring asked, pushing a stack of ten blue chips into the pot.

Joe rolled his eyes and folded, leaving the two aliens the field.

"I'm not sure how to interpret that," the Farling replied, pausing to take a long sip from his beer. Then he reached for the pretzels and held one out to his side, immediately attracting Beowulf, who shouldered the puppies out of the way. "You look like an intelligent dog. What would you do?"

Beowulf thumped down on the floor, rolled on his back, closed his eyes, and let the full length of his tongue dangle out of the side of his mouth.

"Playing dead," the Farling observed. He gave the dog the pretzel and folded his hand. "And so shall I."

"Hey, Beowulf could have seen Dring's cards," Herl protested.

"I have no objection," the Maker said, raking in the pot. "For future reference, M793qK, Beowulf is very intelligent, but he only bets on aces."

"My deal," Joe announced, gathering in the cards. "And here's Walter."

"No Daniel?" Clive asked, as the managing editor of the Galactic Free Press took a seat.

"Kelly cornered him and started quizzing the poor guy about his open worlds," Walter replied. "The rest of the women were polishing off the baked goods, and Shaina was preparing some shower games, so I got out while the getting was good. I must give all due credit to Thomas, though. He's hanging in there and recording everything like some kind of alien anthropologist."

The Farling eyed the newcomer and asked, "Are you the Walter responsible for the crossword puzzles in the Galactic Free Press?"

"No," Walter lied smoothly, taking the seat between Jeeves and Clive. "What have I missed?"

"Doc bet us all that humanity wouldn't pass the Stryx review," Woojin said. "And he called Jeeves a nosy busybody."

"Can I put you down for twenty on the review results?" the Farling inquired.

"I never bet on politics, it's all fixed," the newspaper editor replied. "By the way, Clive. I checked on those reporters you asked about. Two of them are still working for us, and I called them both back to Union Station to be available to give testimony if that's required."

"The reporters you ransomed from pirates?" Herl asked.

"I thought that if the committee is going to do a hearing, I didn't want my sister and the young guy she escaped with to be the only human witnesses," Clive explained. "The Hortens might have accused us of putting them up to it."

Nine

"Can she have cake?" Judith asked the hostess of the baby shower.

"As long as she continues to be a good puppy," Shaina replied, giving the family's recently adopted Cayl hound a smile.

"What's her name?"

"She hasn't chosen it yet. We keep trying new ones on her, and I'll know we've hit the right name if she actually comes when I call her without making me beg."

"Good, Shaina," Brinda cooed, patting her older sister on the head. "Way to show her who's in charge."

"So when do I get to open my presents?" Lynx asked, her eyes on the table piled high with nicely wrapped packages. "Thank you Affie, Flazint," she added, nodding to Dorothy's friends, who added their own gifts to the mound. The two alien girls were attending because they were curious about human rituals and wanted to be prepared if they should ever be called upon to host such an event for the ambassador's daughter.

"After the games," Shaina said. "Have another glass of milk."

"I don't understand why we have to play games," the expectant mother groused.

"Because otherwise it would be cake, presents, and done," Chastity said. She settled onto the couch next to Lynx, cradling her newborn boy in both arms.

"Why do you get a say? You didn't even have a baby shower," Lynx complained.

"I'm rich and I like to do my own shopping," Chastity replied matter-of-factly. "I wouldn't feel comfortable accepting presents from people and then not using them. Hey, Dorothy. Good to see you out and about."

"Do you like my frock? I had the idea months ago but somehow I never got around to it. You won't believe the new shoe prototypes we're working up. I'll bring them by your office next week."

"I gave myself forty days off," the publisher of the Galactic Free Press informed the ambassador's daughter. "Besides, it will be a few weeks before I'm ready to even walk in heels, much less tango."

"All right everybody, gather around," Shaina called out in her auctioneer's bellow. Conversations in the crowded apartment came to a sudden halt, with the exception of Kelly badgering Daniel in a corner about some obscure alien etiquette. "You too, Ambassador. Leave my poor husband alone so he can go play poker."

Kelly reluctantly relaxed her grip on the EarthCent consul's sleeve and joined the crowd around the couch. "Any cake left?"

"I saved you a piece," Donna whispered, handing the ambassador something squishy wrapped in a napkin.

"So the prize for whoever wins the first game is a family dinner at Pub Haggis," Shaina announced. She nodded to her sister Brinda, who began passing out Dollnick stylus boards, a cheap plastic substitute for paper and pencil that could display preloaded text.

"Finish Mommy's Sentence?" Dorothy read out loud.

"I asked Lynx five questions earlier, and the first half of each of her answers is loaded on the Dolly boards. Everybody tries to complete how she responded, and whoever comes the closest wins."

"You didn't tell me that's what the questions were for," Lynx protested. "This is embarrassing."

"No kibitzing," Shaina remonstrated. "Just write in your answers, and when everybody is finished we'll read them out loud."

The women all set to work, a few laughing as they wrote in their guesses.

"This is fun," Molly whispered to her sister-in-law. "Do all of the expectant mothers on Union Station have baby showers like this?"

"I've gone to quite a few for our InstaSitters, but they usually just have a meal at a restaurant," Blythe replied. "It's probably a generational thing."

"All right, is everybody finished?" Shaina asked. "Good. Who thinks they know Lynx's answer to, 'If I had a million creds, I would ____.'"

"Hire a surrogate mother," Chance said confidently.

"Where were you with that answer eight and a half months ago?" Lynx demanded over the laughter.

"That's incorrect," Shaina informed them. "Who else?"

"Buy a twelve year subscription to InstaSitter," Chastity read off her board.

"That's what I had," her older sister and co-founder of InstaSitter complained.

"Me too," most of the women in the room chipped in.

Lynx shook her head. "I hate to sound cheap, especially since I know that InstaSitter funded a good part of my EarthCent Intelligence salary when we started out, but

Thomas already volunteered to come by and babysit whenever Wooj and I need a break."

"You poor fool," Kelly addressed the artificial person, who was moving about in stealth mode recording video of the party.

"I always enjoyed babysitting. And if I'm tied up, my better half is probably available."

"Chance?" Kelly asked incredulously. "To babysit?"

"She's much more responsible than when we first got together," Thomas said defensively. "Besides, Libby can supervise."

"Who else has a good answer?" Shaina called, clapping her hands to regain everybody's attention.

"Acquire a sister wife to change the diapers," Molly suggested.

"Close enough," Shaina declared over an explosion of laughter. "Molly wins. The next partial answer is, 'When I first met my husband, I thought he looked ____'"

"You should have told me it was for a game," Lynx moaned, turning red and burying her face in her hands.

"Korean?" Kelly guessed, not needing to refer to her board.

"Trustworthy," Donna said, having been impressed with Woojin from the first time she met him.

"Desperate?" Chance suggested. Lynx growled and threw a pillow at her.

"Hungry," Blythe said confidently. Shaina pointed a finger at her, as if the co-founder of InstaSitter had placed a winning bid.

"How did you know that?" Lynx demanded.

"My husband mentioned it," Blythe replied. "The first time you saw Wooj was when Joe brought him to meet you and Clive for a recruitment dinner. It was hamburgers and fries at first sight."

"Two down," Shaina announced, and began the next partial sentence. "When my husband and I play poker with my friends, I try to ____."

"Win all of his money," Judith blurted out, having played in one of the Mac's Bones games.

"Keep him from drinking too much beer and staying in every hand," Kelly said.

"I almost told her that," Lynx admitted.

"Keep Beowulf from looking at my cards," Blythe read off her board.

"I *should* have told her that," Lynx said.

"Stay out of pots with Jeeves," Dorothy read off her own Dolly board.

"Come out ahead of Shaina," Brinda proposed.

"Make my husband look good?" Molly guessed.

Shaina kept shaking her head in the negative, and when all the answers were exhausted, she read, "Win enough to cover Woojin's losses."

"Really?" Kelly asked, surprised by the admission.

"He's terrible at poker," Lynx said in exasperation. "All of those ex-mercenaries play their cards rather than the other players. He thinks it's all about betting big on good hands regardless of what everybody else is doing. And I can't teach him anything."

"Your father was a professional gambler," Brinda reminded her. "That's a pretty high standard."

"But Wooj doesn't even try," the expectant mother complained. "He can do statistics in his head and compute the odds for infantry engagements, but when it comes to placing bets and day-to-day living, it's all superstition and instinct. He keeps asking me if I dream about flowers, and

I swear that every time he goes shopping, he comes home with another package of seaweed soup for me to eat after the baby arrives."

"That's sweet," Chastity said.

"But he has more faith in those old Korean traditions than in M7-whatever, the Farling doctor who made it all possible and gave me the watch."

"M793qK," Thomas interjected.

"You're still wearing that novelty countdown watch?" Kelly inquired, unable to hide her skepticism.

"The Farling may be a jerk, but he knows human biology," Lynx replied, glancing at the watch. "Thirteen days, seven hours and forty-two minutes from now I'll be meeting my brown-eyed son."

"I'm sure he was just pulling your leg," the ambassador insisted.

"I've got five creds that says it's accurate within an hour," Lynx said stubbornly.

"I'll put five on four hours early," Chastity took her up. "That's when mine arrived."

"Yeah, but you're always in a hurry," Blythe reminded her sister. "Can I get two hours late?"

"Give me one of those Dolly boards so I can mark these down," Lynx said. After recording the three bets, she looked up and asked, "Anybody else want in the pool?"

"And you all think I'm a spendthrift," Chance interjected. "How can you bet against her when it's her own body?"

"Babies come out when they want to," Donna explained to the artificial person, and then turned to the expectant bookmaker. "I see you as a six-hours-early person."

"So the closest time wins?" Brinda asked. Receiving an affirmative nod, she said, "Give me two days late."

"What?" Lynx squawked, looking up in horror.

"It's strategic," the younger Hadad sister said apologetically.

"And give me two days early," Shaina requested.

Lynx recorded the times and looked to the ambassador for her bet, but Kelly responded indignantly, "I'm not gambling on your delivery time, and I don't understand how you can."

"It's not gambling when it's a sure thing," the cultural attaché retorted confidently.

"Can I get one hour early?" Dorothy requested.

"You should take two hours early," Thomas said. "She wins if she delivers within an hour either way, so you only win if she's between an hour and two hours early."

"I thought you de-integrated your professional gambler upgrade from QuickU," Lynx said accusingly.

"Choosing a time in a delivery pool isn't exactly counting into six decks," the artificial person replied. "And put me down for six hours late."

"Four hours," Molly called out.

"Early or late?" Lynx asked.

"Whichever is open, I forgot."

"One more and it's a fifty-cred pool," Lynx said, peering around the room for takers.

Judith whispered something to Thomas, received a reply, and said, "Give me twelve hours late."

"All right everybody, ante up," Lynx demanded, holding out a hand.

"I want you to know there was no gambling at my shower for you," Kelly reassured her daughter.

"That's great to know, Mom. Can I borrow five creds?"

Shaina handed her own five creds to Brinda to pass along and checked her Dolly board. "Two more Mommy answers."

"Later," Lynx pleaded. "I want to open my presents."

"But what about the gift certificate to Pub Haggis?"

"Just collect all the boards and check the answers."

Shaina sighed and accepted the boards as they were passed back to her, checking the answers as they arrived. "Unbelievable. It's a tie between Blythe and Molly."

"It's a family thing," Blythe boasted, putting an arm around her newly discovered sister-in-law. "I've read Lynx's personnel folder and Molly's a good guesser."

"That one's from me," Dorothy blurted out as Lynx began carefully unwrapping the top present from the pile. "Oh, I forgot she was supposed to guess who gave them," the ambassador's daughter added, glancing in Shaina's direction.

"The fabric is beautiful," the expectant mother marveled, extracting a blue silk garment. "It seems awfully long for a baby, though. Did you order it from a traditional Korean catalog?"

"Were the presents supposed to be for the baby?" Dorothy asked in surprise. "I got it for you. It's a nightgown."

The older women all suppressed their laughter, though there were a few snorts as Lynx held up the slinky garment and gaped at the narrow waist.

"What size do you think I am, Dorothy?"

"Well, you're big now, obviously, but you'll be back to your fighting weight in no time."

"Um, thank you," Lynx said, folding the nightgown and putting it aside in case she fell into a time warp and returned to being sixteen years old.

106

"What's in that one?" Kelly asked, pointing at a large box that sat next to the pile. "I picked it up earlier and it jingled."

"Probably one of those mobiles, to give the baby something to think about," Brinda guessed. "Make sure all of the pieces are strongly attached so they don't fall into the crib."

Lynx worked the lid free and pulled out a bizarre construction that looked a little like an overgrown chandelier. Around the periphery, different lengths of metal chains made out of some super-light alloy hung down, fuzzy balls at the end of each. She held it up and flicked one of the balls with a finger, causing a muffled bell sound.

"Is it a mobile?" Kelly asked, breaking the uncomfortable silence.

"It's a Frunge Fascination," Judith explained enthusiastically. "I got it from Tzurkik's in the Shuk. It's to help the baby develop the hand-eye coordination to become a great swordsman."

"Oh, right," Lynx said, forcing a smile. "That's great. I'm sure Woojin will be thrilled."

Judith beamed proudly and mouthed "Told you so," at Thomas, who had advised his assistant that she was unlikely to find an appropriate baby shower gift at her favorite Frunge weapons dealer.

Lynx reached next for a medium-sized package, gave it an experimental shake, and then pushed the red disc affixed to the top of the ribbon, which released the expensive Dollnick wrapping paper. The box lid popped open to reveal a device that looked like a cross between a small display tab and a handgun.

"Oooh, I looked at those, but they said it wouldn't work for humans," Chastity said.

"Is it some kind of game controller?" Lynx asked.

"It's a Dollnick baby health monitor," Thomas explained. "You point it at the baby and you get all of his vital signs. I reprogrammed it with Libby's help, otherwise everything would have indicated a very sick Dollnick."

"Thank you, Thomas," Lynx said, genuinely touched by the gift. "And thank you, Libby," she added, speaking in no particular direction.

"You're welcome," the station librarian's voice responded. "Open more. I want to see if the rest of my guesses are all correct."

"I'll do this one next," Lynx said, picking up the gift brought by Dorothy's Frunge friend and studying the alien packaging. "How do I open this?"

"Just say, 'open,'" Flazint told her.

"Open," Lynx commanded, but nothing happened.

"I forgot, you have to say it in Frunge," the alien girl added, and then supplied the word herself. The top of the box popped open, revealing a large rock that looked like it suffered from a disease that gave it reddish-orange blemishes.

"What is that?" Dorothy asked her friend.

"It's bauxite," Flazint replied. "It's a traditional baby gift. Don't you guys give ore? Bauxite is rich in aluminum."

"It's the thought that counts," Lynx said graciously, giving the Frunge girl a smile. "And I remember that this one is from Affie." She loosened the drawstring on the velvety Vergallian gift bag and withdrew a small mask made out of some soft alien material. Painted on the mask was the ugliest baby face any of them had ever seen.

"It's for protection," Affie explained in the stunned silence. "Vergallians believe that if a baby is too beautiful,

108

evil spirits will steal it and leave a changeling in its place. The mask fools the evil spirits so they look elsewhere."

"Well it certainly is ugly," Lynx finally said. "Thank you." She reached for the next package and paused, an odd look on her face. "Why does this wrapping paper look so familiar?"

"Was that from you?" Kelly asked. "I try to keep track of who gives us what when I recycle, but you know how it is."

"But this is from the retirement present Wooj and I gave Joe just last week. See all the little wrenches in the pattern?"

"Open it and see if you're getting Joe's gift back," Chastity suggested.

Lynx made a point of ripping off the paper rather than neatly removing it, and then she broke into a broad smile at the present. "I've been searching for one of these forever. Where did you find it?"

"I asked my mother to send it from Earth," the ambassador replied.

"Wouldn't that cost a fortune?" Molly whispered to Blythe.

"Not for Kelly. The Stryx provide a diplomatic pouch service."

"It's just a big empty book with really thick pages," Chastity pointed out, as Lynx paused to clean an imaginary speck of dust off the transparent plastic coating of a page. "Does the baby draw in it?"

"It's a photo album," Kelly explained. "You know that Lynx likes taking pictures with her antique camera, even though the film is expensive and has to be sent to Earth for processing. Joe told me that when he visited his grandmother as a child, she had books and books full of family

109

photographs, some of them so old that they weren't even in color."

"I've been keeping all of my prints in the boxes I get from the lab," Lynx said. "This is really great."

"Joe also said that he remembers some of the cutest were of a baby growing up with a puppy."

Lynx's smile faded in an instant. "Is this a conditional gift?"

"No," Kelly sighed. "No leashes attached."

"Then it's back to being really great," Lynx said happily, putting the photo album aside and reaching for the next package. "Feels fluffy." She found a seam and rapidly removed the wrapping. "Ooh, a handmade baby quilt. Where did you find this?" she asked, looking around.

"I didn't find it," Donna said. "I was already making one for Chastity and I don't know when I'll have another chance to use all the scraps of blue material I begged from everybody."

"But it must have taken forever," Lynx said, trying to remember if she had ever done anything nice for Donna.

"I sew them at work," Donna replied. "You probably didn't notice since I'm usually knitting. It gives me something to do with my hands, and it confuses the alien agents who stop in to spy on us."

Ten

"Welcome to the set of 'Let's Make Friends,'" Aisha addressed the group of schoolchildren and little Stryx. "My daughter, Fenna, has told me about all of the interesting places she's visited with the class to see each of your parents at work. Today you'll get to see two of your classmates working as well. Did the technical assistant give those of you without translation implants an earpiece? Good. We only have twenty minutes before the Grenouthians let in the studio audience, so I'll stop right here and ask if you have any questions. Yes?"

"Who are you?" demanded a little girl in the front.

"Aisha. What's your name? Haven't you ever watched the show?"

"Sylvia. And of course I watch, but you're not Aisha."

"She is too," Fenna defended her mother. "Tell them, Mikey."

"She's Aisha," Mike supported his friend. "Me and Spinner are on the cast, so we know."

"Spinner and I," Aisha corrected him.

"You don't look like her," Sylvia said skeptically. "Your hair is all funny and you're wearing a jumpsuit!"

"I change right before the show so my saris won't get dirty, and the Grenouthian stylist does my hair."

"But you're a lot older than Aisha," a little boy said.

"It's because she's not wearing makeup," Fenna told the boy, happy for a chance to show off her professional knowledge. "She needs it because of the special lighting."

"How come the lighting isn't making the rest of us look old?" the boy persisted, looking around at his classmates.

"Fenna means the lighting for the immersive cameras when I'm on stage," Aisha explained. "When people grow up, our skin isn't as nice as when we were children, and the lighting makes us look even older than we are. Makeup hides that."

"Are you going to put it on so we can see how?" Sylvia asked.

"A Grenouthian artist does my makeup right before the show," Aisha said, and couldn't stop herself from adding, "It only takes a minute because there isn't that much to do. What other questions do you have?"

"Why is the room fake?" a different student challenged her, pointing towards the stage. "It doesn't even have four walls or a ceiling."

"It's what we call a set," Aisha explained. "If there were four walls and a ceiling, the studio audience wouldn't be able to see inside, and the immersive cameras would have to be crowded in the room with us."

"So there's more than one fake room?" another child asked.

"No, we always use the same set."

"That's not a set then. Sets are groups of things, like apples, oranges and bananas, or tall children and short children."

"Oh, you mean sets and numbers, like from Fenna's homework. This is a different kind of set."

"Where are the alien children?" Sylvia asked.

"Where are the other cast members?" Aisha rephrased the question. "They're on their way here by now. Some of them have to wake up very early or stay up very late, since we do the show on human time."

"But Mikey told us you keep them in boxes under the floor," a little Stryx protested.

"Michael Hadad Cohan! Why would you say such a thing?"

"I don't know," the boy mumbled, shrugging at the same time.

"He was probably practicing his imagination," Spinner suggested.

"I want you all to use your imaginations, of course, but not to tell—to make up things like that!"

"How much do you pay?" Sylvia asked.

"Pay?" Aisha turned back to the inquisitive little girl, unsure that she had heard the question properly.

"Mikey and Spinner, for being on your show. With all of the commercials you must make piles of creds. My Dad says that you bought a whole fleet of spaceships."

"I—they were old spaceships, the station manager was getting rid of them," Aisha replied defensively. "My husband and his father will probably take most of them apart to sell the pieces. And we do pay Mike. His parents opened a Stryx account for him and he'll get the money when he grows up."

"You don't pay Spinner?" a different little Stryx asked.

"Er, no. Libby said it would just complicate things if a Stryx was getting paid by the bunnies. I mean, the Grenouthians."

There was an awkward silence, and then a little boy asked, "Who makes up the first line for Storytellers?"

"I do," Aisha said, relieved to finally get a softball question.

"They're really goofy," the boy told her.

"Goofy?" she repeated, her face falling. "But it's everybody's favorite part of the show. The Grenouthian ratings say so."

"The *stories* are good, it's just the beginnings that are goofy," the boy continued his critique. "You should start with space battles or killer robots. Stuff like that."

"But I don't want to give our audience nightmares," Aisha protested. "I put a great deal of thought into those beginnings." She neglected to add that the thought was invested in trying to come up with opening lines that would resist being turned into stories about kidnapped children and ghost battleships, though she rarely succeeded in this.

"Give us an example," a girl demanded.

"Once upon," Sylvia announced.

"A time!" the children and little Stryx shouted.

"There was a young boy who planted a vegetable garden," Aisha responded reluctantly. She wasn't thrilled to be using up one of her stock of future story openers, which she hoped would lead to an upbeat, pastoral tale.

"Who wants to make up a story about vegetables?" the boy who initially raised the subject said in disgust. "My mother makes me eat wax beans, and that gives *me* nightmares."

"But imagine those little seeds starting under the ground and growing into plants that feed us," Aisha urged the children. "You could make up lines about the sun and the rain, and how the little boy..."

"We live on a space station," Sylvia interrupted. "There is no sun or rain."

"They could be alien seeds," Mike suggested.

"That grow into monsters," the young Stryx beside him added.

"Spinner!" Aisha exclaimed. "Where did you get such an idea?"

"From playing Storytellers," Spinner replied. "Libby says that my imagination is almost too good now."

"And when the boy comes to water his vegetables, the monster plants could eat him!" a little girl said excitedly.

"And when the plants finish eating all the people, they can start eating each other," Fenna suggested.

"That's gross," Sylvia said. "Monster plants eating each other?"

"But it's okay for the monster plants to eat children?" Aisha couldn't help asking.

"It's just a story," Sylvia pointed out. "Besides, we eat vegetables, so it's only fair."

A large Grenouthian hopped up to the group and exclaimed, "Oh my fur and whiskers. I'm late. I'm late."

"Are we running behind?" Aisha asked, trying to hide her relief. "I'm sorry, children. I have to get ready now."

"Actually, we're right on time," the assistant director admitted. "I just thought the children would recognize my interpretation of the best character your Earth entertainment industry ever produced."

"The White Rabbit," Fenna cried. "Alice in Wonderland."

The Grenouthian took a bow, and then gave Aisha a nudge towards the backstage area. "And if you don't get ready, you'll be late, be late, for a very important date with a makeup artist and a hair stylist. The rest of the cast is already in wardrobe, but if Mike and Spinner—uh, sorry young Stryx—if Mike, wants to have a bit of refreshment first, the dessert catering you ordered for the children has been set up backstage."

"I hope you all enjoy the show," Aisha called after Fenna's classmates, who were stampeding for the cake and ice cream. "This section of seats is reserved for you, so enjoy your snack and then come back here. Fenna can explain how everything works."

Just fifty minutes later, after the third commercial break, Aisha addressed herself directly to the studio audience.

"Today is a very special day for me, because my daughter and her classmates are in the studio watching our show. We've also reached the end of the current cast rotation, but don't worry. Your favorite friends will be back for another round in a couple of cycles." She turned towards the children on the set and asked, "Does anybody remember what we do on the show before rotating the cast?"

"You ask us all to say what we learned about making friends," the Horten girl answered.

"That's right, Orsilla. Do you want to go first?"

"Do I have to?"

"Oh, I thought you wanted to," Aisha said. "Does somebody else want to go first?"

The Drazen boy raised his tentacle behind his head and waved it like a flag.

"Yes, Pluck?"

"I learned not to tell aliens that they smell bad."

"Smell different," Aisha gently suggested as an alternative. "Did you learn anything else about making friends?"

The Drazen child looked puzzled and then shrugged. "No."

"Okay, who's next?"

116

"Me," the Frunge boy said. "I learned that just because aliens have weird hair and eat funny stuff doesn't make them stupid."

"Thank you, Vzar," Aisha said, hoping that the Frunge word which translated into "stupid" had a softer connotation in languages other than English. "How about you, Krolyohne?"

The Verlock replied ponderously, "Vzar used my answer."

"But you don't have hair," Aisha pointed out. "Oh, I guess I see. Nothing else?"

"Nobody gets my math jokes, except for Spinner."

"Yes, the Stryx are very good at math from the moment they begin thinking," Aisha said. "And what have you learned, Spinner?"

"I think that anybody can be friends with anybody else if they want to be," the little Stryx responded.

"That's very wise of you, Spinner. And you, Clume?"

"I learned how to get up in the middle of the night and miss meals."

"Oh, is it one of those days?" Aisha asked sympathetically.

The Dollnick boy just yawned and scowled.

"I learned that aliens have different rules for everything!" Mike complained.

"Everything?"

"Games and stuff. You know. And every time we play something new, Orsilla makes the rules tricky so she wins."

"But you can still be friends," Aisha said.

"I guess we are, but I wish she'd let somebody else win sometime."

"I'm ready now," Orsilla said suddenly.

117

"Good. What did you learn about making new friends from other species?"

"Aliens don't know how to do anything right, so you have to pretend not to notice if you want them to like you."

"Don't you mean that the other children don't know how to do things like Hortens?"

"That's what I said."

"And we'll be back with our final segment, right after this message from our sponsors," Aisha announced, anticipating the assistant director's signal.

The light on the front immersive camera blinked off, and Clume collapsed dramatically to the floor where he feigned falling asleep.

"You're wasting your energy," Orsilla informed the Dollnick child. "It's the short break. We'll be live in…"

"Five, four, three, two, one," the assistant director counted them back in as Clume scrambled to his feet.

"And welcome back," Aisha said when the front camera went live. "In honor of the end of our current cast rotation, I thought it would be fun for us to see the different ways our new friends think about growing up." She paused for the applause that never materialized because she had forgotten to tell the Grenouthians her plans and nobody turned on the applause sign. "Come on. Everybody sit in a circle and tell us what you think about growing up."

"It's a waste of time," Orsilla said. "I can't wait to be a grownup."

"I'm tired of being told what to do all the time," Vzar chipped in.

"Me too," the other cast members all chorused, including Spinner.

"Is that it? Since we all agree about growing up, can we play a game now?" Orsilla asked.

118

"But that's not—how about telling us what you want to be when you grow up."

"A pirate," Orsilla responded. "But without the tattoos."

"Orsilla! What would your parents say?"

"They won't let me," the little girl admitted. "That's why I have to wait until I'm grown up. My parents say that pirates give Hortens a bad name, but I like that they don't have to follow the rules."

"That's what I want to be too," Mike chimed in. "It's not fair that the Hortens get to be all of the pirates."

"Mike! You can't be serious. Do you know what pirates do?"

"But Mom bought me a pirate uniform, and when I wore it to Fenna's birthday party, you said I was handsome."

"You mean a costume," Aisha said. "People dress up in costumes to play make-believe because it's a different way of using our imaginations. It doesn't mean you want to be a real pirate."

"But I do!"

"Me too," Pluck said, jumping up in excitement. "I don't want to wait for my Name Day to get new toys. And if I was a pirate, I could carry a really big axe and nobody would say I looked funny."

Aisha glanced over at the assistant director, hoping against hope that he would insert an emergency commercial and give her a chance to regroup. The Grenouthian was staring at the real-time ratings monitor in rapt attention, and from his expression, Aisha knew that she could expect no help from that quarter.

"My father told me that pirates are bad for business," the Dollnick boy said, coming out of his lethargy.

119

"You see?" Aisha told the other children. "Pirates take things without paying for them, so the hard working people lose."

"I don't want to be a loser," Clume said, squinting as he gave the matter his sleepy attention. "Maybe I should be a pirate too."

"Children, children. Piracy isn't a game. They—" Aisha paused, unable to see a way to talk about the horrors of piracy to young children. "Spinner. I know that the Stryx elders have asked all of the tunnel network species to band together and defeat the pirates. Can you tell the children why?"

"Clume already said," the young Stryx replied. "Piracy is expensive for people who aren't pirates. But if Mikey and all of my friends want to be pirates when they grow up, I guess I'll have to become a pirate too."

"You can't mean that, Spinner. You'd stop traders in space and, uh, be mean to them? Steal their cargo and hold them hostage for ransom?"

"We get to do all of that?" Mikey interrupted. He bumped forearms with Pluck, the Drazen equivalent of a high five.

"Maybe those pirates are bad pirates," Spinner replied to Aisha's question, his mechanical voice sounding a bit scratchy as he became confused. "We'd be good pirates, and we'd pay for the cargo and invite the passengers to play with us. We could all use our imaginations," he concluded brightly.

"But that's not what pirates do," Aisha objected. Then she realized she was blowing a golden opportunity to close the subject and reversed course. "I mean, if all of you want to grow up to be good pirates, that changes everything.

What would you do if you were a good pirate, Krolyohne?"

"Math," the Verlock girl replied, and then she became excited. "But I wouldn't have to write out the whole proof every time I learned something new. I could just prove the parts that aren't obvious, and maybe," she paused and lowered her voice, "sometimes I'd just come up with answers and not show my calculations."

"I think I understand now," Aisha said. "You all see being pirates as a chance to make up your own rules." She glanced at Vzar, wondering if she should gamble on soliciting his take on piracy before moving on, and to her surprise, she saw that he looked angry. "If nobody else…"

"Pirates are nasty," the Frunge boy said. "When my sister had her first budding party, my parents told me lock up Szroof during the ceremony so she wouldn't jump on the table and eat the meat. Some older shrubs who came dressed as pirates snuck in and ate the best cuts, and Szroof got blamed."

"Szroof?"

"My short-haired desert cat."

Aisha's implant pinged with the one-minute warning, and she rushed to wrap things up. "Next show we'll have a brand-new cast rotation waiting to make friends, including a trio of Fillinducks and our first Vergallian boy. And before we go, I want to thank Stryx Libby for letting my daughter's class come and watch the show today. Ready?"

Behind her, the children formed their traditional double chorus line and whispered amongst themselves, while the Grenouthian sound manager in the booth queued the music to the theme song.

Don't be a stranger because I look funny,
You look weird to me, but let's make friends.
I'll give you a tissue if your nose is runny,
I'm as scared as you, so let's become pirates!

Aisha jerked her head around as the children all shouted their improvised closing, and she saw that Mike and Spinner were holding Vzar's arms, while Pluck held his tentacle over the Frunge boy's mouth.

"That's a wrap," the assistant director called when the light on the front immersive camera blinked out. "Great show. Kids love pirates."

Aisha shook her head in remorse, but she supposed it wouldn't change the galaxy that the children sang the wrong words on purpose this one time. As Fenna ran up and hugged her around the waist, Krolyohne's mother grabbed the Verlock girl by the ear and dragged her away while delivering a ponderous lecture. "You - want - to - solve - math - problems - without – showing- your – calculations - young - Miss? Not - in - my - lifetime, you - won't."

Eleven

"Just a sec," Dorothy called out when she heard the door to the office of SBJ Fashions slide open. "Save it as, uh, work in progress," she instructed the holographic rendering workstation. "And hide it," the young designer added on second thought, just in case the visitor was a spy from a competing fashion business. "I'm in here."

Kevin appeared a moment later, halting in the doorway of the design room. "Are you the only one working?"

"We don't have a full-time receptionist, so unless Shaina and Brinda are hiding in their offices, I'm it at the moment. Now that I think about it, they were taking their kids and the dogs to a park deck today. We have flexible hours."

"How about your alien friends? I thought you said they work with you."

"Flazint and Affie? I'd have to check with Libby to be sure, but I think that Flazint won't be up for another hour or two, and I know Affie went home a little while ago. The Frunge and Vergallians both have longer days than us, so I see a lot of them when we aren't too far out of sync."

"What's with the glitter gloves? You look like a pop star."

"These are Vergallian rendering controllers," Dorothy explained. "I'm not very good with them yet, but they let you create and manipulate holographic images. They're really useful for fashion design. Affie had something

123

similar in her studio for sculpture work, but this system came with built-in dummies for all the species. Wanna see?"

"Sure," the young man said. Dorothy clicked her thumb and middle finger together, a shortcut that brought up a hologram of a gorgeous naked woman, causing Kevin's radiation-tanned face to darken further.

"Are you embarrassed by this?" she asked incredulously. "That's so sweet. It's just a holographic dummy, you know."

"Can't you put something on her?"

"Sure. It works like this." The designer began moving her hands around the hologram, issuing rapid-fire commands as she went. "Straight dress, Drazen tight-weave, number eleven," she instructed the workstation. "Venetian red with standard Horten shoulder puffs—no, down three on the puff, down one more, all right. Gather the waist— no, not in a bunch. Tailor it. Now plunge the neckline, lower, lower, come on, LOWER. That's better. Raise the hem, higher, higher—stop it, you're going to embarrass our guest again."

"It's artificial intelligence?" Kevin asked.

"No, just a good natural language interface. It doesn't really understand half of what I say, but it ignores those parts and carries out the instructions that it knows how to implement."

"And that's all it takes to design a dress?"

"I'm just fooling around with the built-in configurations to learn how it works. This is only fashion designing in the sense that telling a Stryx ship controller to take you somewhere is navigating."

"I get it. So were there some boxes you needed moved around or something? There's no way I can help you with designing clothes."

"What? Oh, right. I asked you to come in to help with something, didn't I?" Dorothy looked around the office, trying to think of some make-work to cover her prior fib, but she came up empty. "My memory is going," she said, furrowing her brow in an attempt to sell the story, but then an idea finally came to her. "I need you for a dummy."

"Excuse me?"

"All of the holographic dummies are women, even the ones with four arms, and the big bunny with the pouch. We design cross-species, you know."

"And I look like some sort of alien female?"

"Silly," she said, casting a coquettish glance over her shoulder as she rummaged in a cupboard. "Jeeves has been pushing me to design something for males since he says you're half the potential market. Just goes to show how little he really knows about biologicals. Anyway, the girls and I want to come up with something unisex that we can sell to anybody."

"Doesn't that just mean a jumpsuit or a shirt and pants?" Kevin asked. "Lots of the independent traders I've met were women, at least the humans, and they mainly dressed just like me."

"Skirts aren't terribly practical in Zero G, if you hadn't noticed. But if you think pants are shaped the same for men and women, you just aren't looking in the right places," she teased, bringing some of the blood back to his face.

"So what exactly do you need me to do?"

"Just take your clothes off so I can get some holo-measurements," she deadpanned, and then laughed outright at his look of horror. "Oh, you're so easy. Jeeves would have a field day with you."

"I'm beginning to suspect you don't have any work for me at all," Kevin said, trying not to sound like a bad sport.

"I just wanted to see you," Dorothy admitted. "You used to follow me everywhere, after all. You and Metoo, both."

"I don't remember," Kevin protested, feeling foolish. But on seeing her smile slip, he added, "I mean, I remember following you everywhere. I just don't remember why."

"Ahem," Jeeves said, floating into the room. "I couldn't help catching the end of your conversation. Unlike some station librarians we know, I try to ignore all of the sound waves bouncing around, but I heard my name."

"I was just warning Kevin about your sense of humor," Dorothy explained.

"I'm sure that a young man intelligent enough to escape from pirates and activate a Verlock rescue device without English instructions can take care of himself." Jeeves turned and directly addressed the embarrassed visitor. "I believe she was implying that you are gullible, a nonexistent condition that has no equivalent expression in any advanced cultures."

"Really?" Kevin asked.

Dorothy laughed again, and slapped the Stryx's casing. "Stop it. That joke was old when Dring was a kid, if Makers are ever young."

"I just thought I'd look in and see if you remembered how to work," Jeeves continued, turning back to Dorothy. "It seems like it was only four months ago that you con-

126

vinced me to purchase this expensive holographic rendering system, and I was beginning to wonder if you ever intended to use it."

"I'm back now, Jeeves. You don't have to keep repeating yourself like a distress signal. And I was just discussing fashion design for men with Kevin, which I seem to recall was your idea. I'm thinking of doing a special line for traders, since the men and women dress the same in Zero G," she improvised. "And they go everywhere and work in public markets, so it would mean maximum brand exposure, just like my InstaSitter idea."

"Interesting," the Stryx said, looking Kevin up and down as if he was seeing the young man for the first time. "Is this your official trader garb?"

"Uh, I probably wear the jumpsuit more, since so many species keep their space stations and orbitals on the cool side. Anywhere warm I go with jeans and a T-shirt." He paused, feeling exceedingly awkward about being called upon to discuss fashion, but wanting to come through for Dorothy. "The jumpsuit is better for working because of the extra pockets up top, and, uh, T-shirts can pull out of your pants when you're twisting around the cargo area in Zero G."

"I see," Jeeves said, though something in his voice conveyed the sense that he was talking about more than fashion. "Well, this will come as welcome news to Joe and Paul since all they wear is jeans, T-shirts and jumpsuits. And I understand that you'll be working with them for the time being."

"Really?" Dorothy interrupted, her eyes shining. "That's great. I'll have you around as a guinea pig for my designs."

127

"The ambassador said that the Verlocks are insisting on giving me a cash payment for the radiation exposure caused by their rescue device, even though it saved our lives," Kevin explained. "It won't be enough to buy a new trader to replace the one the pirates took from me, though. Paul offered to let me pick something I can make space-worthy from his lot in return for whatever the Verlocks pay and helping out until they get everything under control."

"You haven't been to see me, I mean Union Station, in fifteen years, and now you plan on running off again as soon as you have a ship?" Dorothy asked in dismay.

"That's not accurate," Jeeves corrected her. "Kevin visited the station several times after acquiring his two-man trader. Well, I need to be getting along," the Stryx concluded after dropping this bombshell, and shot out of the room.

"It's not like that," Kevin protested to the stricken girl. "I mean, I did come to Union Station, but the first time I went to Mac's Bones, I saw you heading towards the lift tube holding hands with some guy, and you looked right past me. I asked the station librarian about you every time I came back after that, but she said you were still seeing him."

"Libby!" Dorothy practically shouted. "Why didn't you tell me?"

"Kevin asked me not to and I respected his privacy," the station librarian's voice replied.

"Now I feel guilty," the girl complained. "I wish you had come to see me. You must have felt so lonely coming all the way here and not talking to anybody."

"Traveling from place to place without a partner in a two-man trader is always lonely," Kevin replied matter-of-factly. "I picked up some profitable cargoes here which helped me pay off my ship mortgage a few years early, though the timing couldn't have been worse," he added with a grimace. "Trust me. The only thing I regret about my visits to Union Station was losing the Frunge pocket knife that my dad bought me after the Kasilian auction."

"How did that happen?"

"I kind of got drunk for the first and last time after I saw you with that guy, and I think it must have slipped out of my pocket when I was sleeping it off on the park deck. I didn't even realize it was gone until I was in the tunnel on my way to Drazen space."

"So you never went by the station lost-and-found?" Dorothy seized Kevin's hand and began dragging him towards the door. "Come on, I have an in there."

"But that was years ago. They wouldn't keep stuff that long."

"Are you kidding? The Stryx wait like six thousand years to auction off the unclaimed stuff. See this bracelet?" she demanded, holding up her free arm to display the odd alien artifact. "I found it on an empty shelving unit that had already been cleaned out. It's my good luck charm, and it saved me from a gullible alien who thought I was a witch."

"Come again?" Kevin asked, as Dorothy herded him into a lift tube.

"Lost-and-found," she told the capsule before continuing her story. "I was flying around the Physics Ride with David—I'll take you there—and some aliens who were here for the station open house picked a fight with us. Later, one of them came to the lost-and-found to kidnap me, but when he saw the bracelet, he ran away. Do you

129

know what? My brother just started working at the lost-and-found last week and I think he's there now."

The capsule came to a halt, and Dorothy led Kevin down the corridor, regaling him with her lost-and-found stories about funny aliens.

"And you met your ex-boyfriend there?" Kevin asked when she finally let him get a word in edgewise.

"Yes, and Flazint too. She trained me." Dorothy turned into the lost-and-found and skidded to a halt when she saw a giant Dollnick at the end of the counter arguing with Samuel. "Figures," she muttered to Kevin. "I was going to shout 'Fire!' or something, but there's a customer here. Probably the first one he's had in an hour."

"It's not very busy?"

"Most visitors who lose stuff on the station get it returned to them automatically when Libby checks the security imaging," Dorothy explained. "The passenger liners all take lost stuff for delivery gratis, so the things that end up on the shelves are mainly items from station residents and small ship owners without a fixed mailing address."

"Wouldn't it be easier to return lost items to station residents than to travelers who are just passing through?"

"Sure, but the degree of difficulty means nothing to the Stryx. They just don't want station residents to turn the maintenance bots into a maid service, or everybody would get really lazy and leave things wherever."

"That Dollnick looks pretty angry," Kevin said, maneuvering his way in front of the girl as they started for the other end of the long counter.

"Maybe my brother doesn't believe him," Dorothy said. "Sometimes when visitors find out about the lost-and-found, they show up and try to guess stuff that might be here, thinking that they might get something for free. I remember a Sharf who came in once, spent like a half an hour working his way down the outside of the counter staring at the shelves, and then tried to convince me that he had lost a…"

"I demand to see the management!" the Dolly trilled, drowning out Dorothy's words. "How dare you lie to me?"

"A gentleman does not lie, sir," the teenage boy replied in a steely tone. "If you are looking for satisfaction, we must arrange for our seconds to meet and discuss the details."

"Samuel McAllister!" Dorothy shouted, sounding very much like their mother when she was upset. "You are not arranging a duel with this Dollnick."

"But he called me a liar," Samuel replied, his poise remarkable for a fifteen-year-old who had just challenged a four-armed alien more than twice his size. "My honor is at stake."

"You've been watching way too many Vergallian dramas," retorted his sister, who had spent most of the last three months in bed or on the couch doing exactly that. She pushed past Kevin and confronted the towering Dollnick. "The lost-and-found is operated directly by the Stryx, and as a former employee here, I should warn you that the station manager will drop a maintenance bot on your head if you get out of line."

"But this is preposterous," the Dollnick blustered, trapped between an alpha-male culture that demanded a confident display, and the knowledge that maintenance bots were immune to such posturing. "I mislaid a data crystal containing plans for modifying the plumbing on W-class prospecting ships, the commercial value of which is inestimable."

"And you found it, Samuel?"

"Yes, but that's not the only thing on the data crystal," the boy said, looking uncomfortable for the first time. "I put it on the easy round to confirm the contents, and there was a hologram of…"

"Family and friends enjoying a little recreation," the Dollnick interrupted. The pitch of his speech had reached so high that had there been any crystal goblets nearby, they surely would have shattered. "I fail to see what the one has to do with the other."

"Libby said it was pirated video, but the crystal is locked to prevent erasure," Samuel continued. "I gave the Dollnick the choice of unlocking it or supplying a new crystal for the system to transfer the plumbing plans."

"What I choose to view and how I obtain it is none of your business, you Human twerp!" the Dolly shouted, thumping the counter with all four fists. As Dorothy had predicted, a pair of maintenance bots appeared out of nowhere and bracketed the angry alien.

"It's not my call, sir," Samuel replied with dignity. "When I was hired by this establishment I agreed to work according to the rules. We are prohibited from returning pirated content when it comes to our attention."

"But it only came to your attention because you went looking for it," the Dollnick whined, his attitude having done an about-face with the appearance of the bots. "It's true that I brought the data crystal to the station for a meeting, but it actually belongs to my boss. What is he going to say if I bring it back without his private collection? He'll blame me for having left it behind in my room in the first place."

"I'm sorry, but rules are rules," the teenager replied. "You can appeal directly to the station manager, of course, but..."

"No need, no need," the Dollnick muttered, looking a bit sheepish. "Here. Transfer whatever you can onto my personal crystal and keep that one. I'll tell my boss where he can find it."

Samuel quickly carried out the operation and replaced the data crystal on the shelf. "You can inform your superior that it will be filed at location LEV 18/7," he informed the customer. "The data will be waiting for him the next five thousand and eight hundred years or so."

The maintenance bots disappeared, and the giant Dollnick fumbled around for a moment, replacing his personal data crystal in a belt pouch. Then he slapped a coin on the counter and stalked out.

"Hey, a two-cred piece. I didn't know the Stryx even made these," Samuel said.

"I can't believe he gave you anything after all that, but I see two-cred coins out on the frontier a lot," Kevin observed. "That would buy a good dinner on some of the alien stations, or a bed for the night on most rocks, but things are expensive around here."

"So I hear you're working with my Dad and Paul," Samuel said conversationally. "Did you know that Dorothy..."

"Shut up," she interrupted her younger brother, giving him a death stare. "We're looking for a Frunge pocket knife that Kevin lost here, like, how many years ago?"

"Seven-ish," the trader replied. "It had my initials carved into the handle."

"Kevin Crick," Dorothy added.

Samuel waved his hand over the easy round to activate the system, and requested, "Frunge pocket knife with English initials carved in the handle, lost around seven years ago."

"Frunge pocket knife located at JU 3/22," the reply came immediately.

"Cool, this will be my first real retrieval," Samuel said. "The only stuff I've returned so far came from the bins under the counter." He walked along the shelves checking the location readouts and soon found the proper unit. "Top shelf," he ordered, and the plate at the base of the shelving unit began lifting him up towards the ceiling.

"That looks kind of hazardous," Kevin commented.

"There's a force field or something so you can't fall off," Dorothy told him. "I really enjoyed working here," she added wistfully. "And I learned a lot by looking at how alien fashions changed over the last few thousand years."

"Got it," Samuel called out. The lift returned him to the deck where he waved off Kevin's extended hand and headed back towards the easy round. "I've got to check it out."

"Frunge pocket knife with English initials from location JU 3/22," the lost-and-found cataloging system confirmed. "Shall I remove it from inventory?"

"Yes," Samuel replied, passing the knife over the counter to its owner.

"Am I happy to have you back," Kevin exclaimed, prying open a short blade with an oddly shaped notch near the tip. "I don't know what the Frunge use this one for, but it opened cans like it was cutting through paper."

"Do you want me to check and see if Libby has the security imaging from when the knife was lost?" Samuel asked.

"No thanks," Kevin said hastily, slapping a coin on the counter and dragging Dorothy towards the exit.

"Don't you dare get into any duels or I'm telling Dad on you," the girl shouted back at her younger brother.

Twelve

Kelly paused in the corridor and nervously smoothed her dress before entering the Drazen embassy. The mandatory review meetings with the other tunnel network species didn't have to be scheduled in any particular order, and after consultation with Libby, Donna had arranged for the EarthCent ambassador to start with friends who would go easy on her. Although Kelly knew that the Stryx were unlikely to give any great weight to the opinions of the advanced species, she couldn't help feeling a little nervous about having to go out of her way to solicit criticism.

"The ambassador just finished a holo-conference and he's waiting for you," the Drazen receptionist informed Kelly. "You know the way to his office."

"Yes, thank you."

The embassies maintained by the aliens all made the EarthCent embassy seem like a storage closet in comparison, but that was because the advanced species rented space using their own budgets. The door to Bork's office was open, and Kelly entered the familiar space with its décor of battle axes and medieval-style weaponry.

"Ambassador," Bork greeted her, rising rapidly to his feet and coming around the desk. "Can I get you anything? A drink?"

"I better not, thank you," Kelly replied. "You're my first meeting of the day."

"I understand," Bork replied cheerfully, bypassing the hidden bar and returning to his seat, since Drazen etiquette didn't allow for drinking alone. "I hope you aren't nervous. Keep in mind that none of us on Union Station have participated in a species review, so you know as much about it as we do."

"That's what makes me nervous," Kelly replied with a forced laugh. "From what I understand, I'm supposed to ask you to tell me honestly what bothers you about humanity."

"Really?" Bork tilted his head, shut one eye, and scratched behind an ear with his tentacle. "But I have the highest regard for your people, and I consider you a close friend."

"I didn't mean that you're supposed to complain about me, Bork," Kelly said, though she couldn't help but feel warmed by the alien ambassador's words. "Libby wouldn't go into detail about what the point of these encounters is supposed to be, but I tried to prepare by asking actors employed by EarthCent Intelligence to pose a number of questions about topics we think might be bothering you."

"That sounds very interesting. What did you learn?"

"Nothing," Kelly admitted. "Well, the Frunge aren't crazy about our deck lighting, but I guess that's normal for them. I just had the feeling that the actors were all holding back from telling me what was really on their minds."

"Well, most of your food is pretty bland," the Drazen ambassador offered. "Does that help?"

"Now you're doing it too," Kelly accused him. "Come on. I'm sure there are things about humans driving you nuts that can't be fixed with hot sauce. How can we improve if you don't tell us?"

"What if I ask what you don't like about Drazens, and you say that tentacles or second thumbs are offensive? Getting along with other species is just like getting along with other people. You have to accept the bad with the good."

"I know that, Bork. But I'm afraid if I don't get something from you, the Stryx will think that we aren't taking the process seriously."

"I suppose you have a point," the Drazen ambassador allowed. "I did try digging through our archives to see if I could learn anything about prior reviews, but I came up blank."

"So go on, hit me," Kelly demanded.

"I only tell you this under protest, and I ask that with the exception of your report submission to the Stryx, it doesn't go beyond our ears."

"Agreed," the EarthCent ambassador said confidently.

Bork let out a long sigh, then looked Kelly directly in the eye, and said, "It's your singing."

"My singing? As in, me?"

"No, no," the Drazen reassured her. "It's most of humanity. Your professional singers have talent, and the travel choir drawn from Human workers on our open worlds is a pleasure to hear. But your people sing at inappropriate times without giving the music their full attention. And there's scientific evidence that a segment of your population can neither hear nor accurately reproduce relative pitch."

"You're saying we're tone deaf?"

"In comparison to Drazens, I'm afraid many of you are. And that atrocity of a song you insist on screeching at your nativity anniversaries..."

"Happy Birthday?"

"Just hearing it spoken gives me the shivers."

"But I invite you to all of our birthday parties and you always have a good time."

"I just move my lips and play white noise over my implant at top volume while you're all singing," Bork admitted. "Then there's the drinking songs."

"Joe picked those up during his mercenary service, but I try to stop him if he's had a few."

"Actually, most humans sound better when they're inebriated, there's more emotional color," Bork said. "And whistling while you work? I have yet to meet the Human who can effectively multi-task at the required level."

"I, uh, thank you, Ambassador," Kelly pronounced stiffly. "I know how seriously Drazens take music. I guess I just didn't realize that you found our primitive attempts so offensive."

"See? Now you're upset, I knew this would happen. Are you sure you won't take that drink?"

"I'm not upset with you, Ambassador." Kelly rose from her chair and inclined her head briefly. "I'm afraid I have an appointment with Czeros, who sings like a tree groaning in the wind, if you recall. I'll be sure to pass your criticism along to the Stryx."

"Kelly! Wait," Bork said, rising from his chair, but she was already out the door. Rather than giving chase, he pinged the Frunge ambassador over his implant. "Czeros, it's me. Kelly pushed me to give her something serious, so I mentioned their singing, and she left in a huff. What? No, I'm not a complete idiot. All right, we'll talk later."

By the time the EarthCent ambassador reached the lift tube, she was beginning to feel bad about stalking out of Bork's office. After all, she had practically begged him to say something insulting, and the truth was, she could barely carry a tune herself.

"Frunge embassy," she told the capsule. "And Libby, I'm sure you already know, but my official review finding is that the Drazens find our singing offensive."

"Duly recorded," the Stryx librarian replied. "You're going to arrive at the Frunge embassy a half an hour early if you continue on directly. It appears to me that the Grenouthian ambassador is currently unoccupied, and I suspect he's as anxious as you are to get this meeting out of the way. Would you like to swing by the Grenouthian embassy now, and I'll let you know when you have to leave to see Czeros?"

Kelly only had to think for a second. "Yes. That's great if he'll see me now. I'll have an excuse to leave if he brings out a whole laundry list of complaints."

"Rerouting your capsule to the Grenouthian embassy," Libby reported, adding a moment later. "Appointment confirmed."

When the lift tube door opened, Kelly headed directly into the Grenouthian embassy, which was just across the corridor. A number of young bunnies on a school tour stared with eyes bulging from curiosity as she made her way to the reception desk. She was intercepted by a guard wearing a silver sash.

"Follow me," the officious Grenouthian ordered. Kelly was about to say that she knew the way, but she quickly realized that the path she had taken when she recently visited the embassy with Aisha to witness a contract had been changed. The dense hedges that broke up the floor space had apparently been uprooted and replanted in new configurations, and she couldn't help wondering what the Frunge would make of the dim overhead lighting. After a final turn, Kelly suddenly found herself standing in front of the familiar bunny's desk.

"You are late," the Grenouthian ambassador announced.

"How can I be late?" Kelly protested. "Libby just arranged this meeting two minutes ago."

"Two hundred heartbeats early is on time," the ambassador stated. "On time is late, and a hundred heartbeats further along is as good as not showing up. You have come to hear abuse."

"What? No, I mean, sort of. Are you saying I'm not really late?"

"I checked our diplomat records for prior Stryx reviews, so I know you are here to solicit my negative impressions of your species," the ambassador said, ignoring his guest's question. "Humans are rife with deficiencies, but it would be rude for me to point any of them out when I own a very valuable point in 'Let's Make Friends,' thanks to you and your former assistant."

"I forgot that the show was your idea," Kelly said, trying to regain her mental footing. "Since you looked up the history of the Stryx reviews, you must know that politeness is uncalled for in this situation. Please just tell me the truth."

"As you wish," the ambassador replied with a shrug. "How many of your failings shall I recount?"

"I'm not interested in my personal failings, I mean, not right now, anyway. I want to hear what issues you have with my species as a whole."

The Grenouthian stared at her, drumming his hands on his belly while he gave the issue some thought. Finally, he shook his head like a team captain refusing a signal sent in by a coach from the sidelines, and asked, "Who matches orange with blue?"

"Excuse me?"

"I consider myself a well-educated individual with broad taste in art, but pairing colors like red and green or yellow and purple? When I visited your home, the artwork you displayed triggered my regurgitation reflex before I could find the waste facility. I was forced to unload my lunch in what appeared to be a receptacle for dirty clothes."

"You were the one who threw up in my laundry hamper? I remember that. And you say it was because you didn't like my reproductions of the impressionists? Renoir, Monet and Van Gogh are my artistic heroes!"

"Reproductions? You mean there are more of them out there?" The ambassador's short white fur stood on end. "I suppose I shouldn't make such a big deal about it since I know that your species has difficulty detecting contrast. A studio engineer once told me it has to do with the poor sensitivity of your photoreceptors. I understand that you can't even discern colors at moderate lighting levels."

"So first we're tone deaf and now we're color blind?" Kelly would have risen from her chair if the ambassador had provided one, but instead she simply turned on her heel and stalked out through a space in the hedge.

"Not that way," the ambassador called after her. "They're watering."

Kelly rushed through the sprinkler, realized that she was lost, and recalling what Joe had once told her about mazes, began making left turns at every opening. After surprising several young bunnies who were smoking something from a hookah, she gave up and subvoced Libby for help.

"Continue straight until the third opening and then turn right," the Stryx librarian instructed her. "Now stay in the center of the track until the fourth opening on the left…good…your immediate right…and there."

Kelly emerged in the reception area, damp, but relieved she hadn't required a rescue from the Grenouthians. Back in the lift tube, she gave the Frunge embassy for her destination, and then asked Libby, "How come turning left every time didn't work?"

"It would have, eventually, but it's only a method of last resort. I brought you out of the maze using the most direct route."

"Ah, I get it. Libby, the Grenouthian ambassador said that my art made him sick."

"Duly noted. Czeros is still in a meeting, but he always finishes early."

"Because early is on time," Kelly parroted.

"That would be the general sentiment shared by the advanced species."

After she'd exited the lift tube, the ambassador strolled casually down the corridor of the Frunge deck, looking at boutique displays. By the time she reached the embassy, Czeros was just seeing off a Horten, who was wearing a suit that probably cost more than Kelly earned in a year. The Horten looked right through her as they passed, but the Frunge ambassador appeared to be genuinely pleased to see her.

"Unpleasant fellow, that advocate," Czeros commented as he led Kelly to his office. "Has he been around to see you yet?"

"No. Who is he?"

"A paid representative for the main pirate organization on the Sharf/Horten frontier."

"You mean a lobbyist?"

"That's another way of putting it, I suppose, though from his presentation, it's clear that his background is in litigation. I'm afraid we'll be seeing more of him in the future."

"I'm not even thinking about the piracy issue right now. I was recently told that humans have no talent for multi-tasking," Kelly replied sarcastically.

"I suspect it's been a long day for both of us," Czeros said. As soon as they reached his office, he poured the EarthCent ambassador a glass of wine over her objection that it was still morning on human time. He drained his own glass and refilled it before asking, "How can I help you with the review?"

"You're supposed to tell me about any issues the Frunge have with humanity. The Stryx refused to give us details about what to expect, so I prepared on the assumption that the other species would complain about trade issues, the special toll structure for Earth products, things like that. Instead, it seems that the fundamental problem is who we are."

"I'm sure that's not case," Czeros said, sipping his wine. "I find humans to be fine company, and I've heard nothing but good things from Vrazel, who moved his wing-set factory to your world."

"Thank you, Czeros," Kelly said, allowing herself to relax a little and taking a sip of the wine, which was an Earth export. "The truth is, I feel a little bad about the way I left Bork's office after he told me that the Drazens take issue with our singing."

"Complaining about singing does seem a bit petty," said the Frunge ambassador, who had aspired to becoming a vocalist in his youth. "If he had to pick on something,

144

you'd think it would be the odor, since their sense of smell is so much more acute than our own."

"Odor?"

Czeros stiffened like a tree, and then he nervously re-filled his glass even though it wasn't empty yet. "I hear that your cultural attaché is expecting a baby and I have a budget to purchase small gifts for alien diplomats. Perhaps you could help me pick something out?"

"What odor, Czeros?"

"It's really a small matter, not worth mentioning at all," the Frunge diplomat protested. "I believe Lynx mentioned her child will be a boy, so I was thinking about something in the way of…"

"WHAT ODOR, CZEROS?"

The alien ambassador slumped in his chair and knuckled his forehead, apparently feeling the need to apologize in advance for what he was about to say.

"It's not entirely unpleasant, really. Humans give off a characteristic scent that reminds one of, uh, the forest in the spring."

"Oh, that's good, then. You mean like buds and flowers?"

Czeros shook the wine bottle over his glass, trying to coax out a few more drops, and muttered something under his breath that sounded to Kelly like, "regeneration, cycle of life, creating warmth."

"Wait a minute. Are you talking about dead leaves and rotting vegetation?"

"It's a bit strong in crowds, but I just use my filter plugs," Czeros admitted. "The truth is, I find your natural odor easier on the nose than some of the artificial scents your people put on to try to attract one another."

"We stink? And we stink worse when we try not to stink?"

"You're taking this entirely the wrong way," Czeros protested. He reached across the desk for Kelly's hand, but she had already lurched to her feet.

"Thank you for the wine and the feedback, Ambassador. I'd stay to chat, but I wouldn't want to prolong your suffering."

"Kelly!" Czeros called after the departing ambassador. "I'll put in my nose plugs. Oh, grains," he swore, and then spoke at the communications device integrated in his UV desk lamp. "Get me Bork. Bork? I blew it. Yeah, I let something slip about the smell. What? No, I wouldn't bring up the other thing under torture. All right. You ping Crute and I'll try to talk some sense into Abeva. I don't know, maybe she'll keep her mouth shut in return for supporting the Vergallian position in this piracy mess."

By the time Kelly reached the lift tube, she was feeling utterly deflated. "Take me home," she instructed the capsule, before reporting in to the Stryx librarian. "Libby. The Frunge think we smell bad."

"Duly noted. Are you giving up for the day? You're almost halfway through the feedback section of the review, and I can get you in with the Vergallian ambassador if you'd like."

"The new one? I've forgotten her name already."

"Abeva."

"You know what? She's the one I've been dreading the most, so let's get this over with."

"Appointment confirmed, rerouting your capsule."

"Is all of this really necessary, Libby? You must have known what objections the other species were going to raise, and none of it is stuff we can do anything about."

"Good luck with Abeva," the omnipresent Stryx replied.

Kelly exited the capsule and turned down the corridor towards the Vergallian embassy. The last time she had been there it was to accompany the Lood emissary from the Cayl Empire, who had spat a stream of some substance on the ornate doors. Perhaps the Vergallians had learned something from that episode because the doors were wide open when she arrived.

"The ambassador is in her office," a bored looking Vergallian male manning the reception desk informed her. "Oh, you have to check your weapons."

"I don't have any," Kelly replied, rather taken aback by the demand.

"Not even an honor dagger?" the Vergallian asked. "You can keep that, you know. I'm just curious."

"No, I don't carry a dagger. Why would I need weapons on a Stryx station?"

"Interesting," the receptionist commented. "Down the hall to the large gold door at the end."

Kelly found the ambassador's office without a problem, but the door was closed. She wasted a minute looking for a buzzer, then tried an experimental rap with her knuckles, but it was like knocking on the door of a bank vault. Unwilling to return to the reception desk, she subvoced for help.

"Libby? Can you ping Abeva for me without her knowing that you did it? Otherwise, all I'll get out of her is a lecture on us being Stryx pets."

"She'll wonder how you cracked her code," the Stryx said, sounding amused. "Bypassing the Vergallian security layers and patching you through."

"Ambassador?" Kelly's implant did an excellent job translating the note of surprise in Abeva's voice. "I don't recall giving you my personal access code."

"I'm sure you're aware of my ties to EarthCent Intelligence," Kelly subvoced in reply. "I just arrived at your office but the door is closed. Early is on time, you know."

The door opened inward, and Kelly strode into the Vergallian ambassador's office. The décor was surprisingly utilitarian, with the exception of lifelike paintings of the three most beautiful toddlers that the EarthCent ambassador had ever seen. She couldn't help wondering if the portraits were reproductions from some famous Vergallian artist.

"Be seated." Abeva spoke without rising and pointed to the chair in front of her desk. "I understand you are here gathering criticisms for the Stryx."

"I've visited the Drazens, Grenouthians and Frunge already this morning, and I thought I'd get you out of the way while I'm already in a bad mood." Even as the words were coming out, Kelly couldn't believe what she was saying. It was as if she had been drugged, or—"Did you just dose me with pheromones?"

"My office, my rules," Abeva replied sweetly. "Nothing harmful, I assure you. I just thought I'd save myself a little trouble trying to wade through your diplomatic twaddle and get to the truth. It sounds to me like you are displeased with the assessments so far."

"I've been told that humans smell bad, have no artistic sensibility, and can't carry a tune," Kelly heard herself saying before she could consider her response. "What would you like to add to the list?"

"Well, well. It appears that honesty is the order of the day on Union Station." Abeva placed her elbows on the

148

desk, bridged her hands together, and regarded Kelly over the steeple formed by the fingers. "You lack grace."

"What? Are you talking about religious salvation or physical coordination?"

Abeva frowned in frustration. "You also lack a workable language for carrying out intelligent conversations. Obviously I'm talking about physical grace. Just look at the way you're sitting! It's a miracle that you aren't all crooked from bad posture by the time you reach middle age."

"Slouching feels wonderful, not that you'd ever know," Kelly replied pugnaciously. "It beats walking around like you have a broom handle..."

"You're right," Abeva interrupted. "I wouldn't know. But I have heard that Astria's Academy of Dance has already enrolled millions on your Earth, and that the instructors are forced to spend valuable lesson time teaching the students how to walk properly before they can start on basic dance steps. I'll have to remember to send them a suggestion to offer a course on how to sit up straight."

"My son and his partner placed fifth in the Regional Vergallian Ballroom Dancing competition last cycle," Kelly retorted. "And they don't practice eight hours a day, either."

"I'm well aware of the achievements of your son and Vivian Oxford," Abeva replied with a tight smile. "We are not without our own intelligence service, and I've been briefed on your son's connection with young Queen Ailia. Our chief dance analyst has reviewed the competition video and has staked his reputation that Queen Ailia is somehow teaching your son advanced ballroom techniques through an unknown communications technology."

"Your intelligence service has a dance analyst?"

"Your intelligence service doesn't have dance analysts?" Abeva sounded even more surprised than she had when Kelly reached her with a direct ping. "It's one of our larger departments. In any case, the grace displayed by your son and his partner just proves that the rest of you are capable of doing better, which makes it even more irritating. The other species sometimes mistake Humans for Vergallians, and your sloth reflects badly upon us. Couldn't you at least practice walking at home with a book on your head?"

The ambassador sounded so sincere in her criticism that Kelly couldn't help feeling a little ashamed, though perhaps that was an effect of the pheromones as well.

"As long as we're being honest with one another, is there anything about humans you don't find objectionable?"

Abeva stood and walked slowly to the three portraits displayed on the wall. "You mentioned that one of the ambassadors accused you of having bad taste in art. What do you make of these?"

"They're so beautiful," Kelly said, unable to control her tongue. "I thought maybe they were reproductions that were sold with the frames."

The Vergallian ambassador laughed until tears began running down her perfectly sculpted face. "No, they're my children. Our tradition is to have portraits painted for presentation to the mother at the second naming ceremony. My oldest girl is on her third or fourth career—I lose track—and my son is in the Imperial Fleet, but Aciva recently turned three," she concluded, bestowing a gentle air-pat on the blonde hair of the most recent portrait. "It's a difficult age for Vergallian children."

"She looks like a little angel," Kelly said honestly.

"Yes, I suppose she does. You asked me if there is anything about Humans which I don't find objectionable. Before moving from my world to Union Station, I would have been forced to disappoint you, but I've discovered there is one Human innovation for which I thank the stars."

"Disposable diapers?" Kelly guessed.

"InstaSitter."

Thirteen

Thomas approached the open hatch of the old Grenouthian lifeboat where Joe, Paul, and Kevin were puzzling over a device resembling an oversized candelabrum made of quartz.

"Can I borrow Kevin for a few minutes?" Thomas asked, leaning into the opening.

"We're just waiting around for Jeeves to come tell us if we can break this thing down without blowing a hole in the station," Joe replied. "If you need a hand with something, Paul or I can come along as well."

"I just wanted to introduce Kevin to somebody, plus pitch him on the Lynx thing," the artificial person said. "And you know we can always use more stringers."

"What's a stringer?" Kevin asked, swinging himself out of the opening.

"Sort of a casual spy," Thomas explained. "It doesn't rise to the level of part-time work, and there's no regular income, though EarthCent Intelligence will subsidize your expenses if you add certain destinations to your trading itinerary. It's mainly about knowing who to contact if you come across anything of strategic interest, how to recognize important developments, plus a little tradecraft for communications."

"And what's with the lynx you mentioned?" Kevin looked around cautiously as they strolled towards the training camp area. "I have a hard time believing that Beowulf would tolerate a wildcat in Mac's Bones."

"Lynx was the first human agent recruited by EarthCent Intelligence. She and I were partners until we got promoted out of the field. Lynx was a trader for ten years before joining up, and she's always handled that part of the training for us, but she'll be out on maternity leave when the next class of recruits starts through the camp. Blythe told me that you've been on the trading circuit for practically your whole life, so we thought you might be willing to do a bit of teaching. We pay top dollar for adjunct faculty."

"I've never taught anything," Kevin admitted. "Everything I know about galactic politics and military alliances I learned from reading the Galactic Free Press."

"Don't worry about any of that. Your job would be teaching them the basics of trading, starting from blanket etiquette, on up through how to drive a bargain. An agent who can't make a profit trading may as well skip the cover story altogether."

"Maybe I could do that much. Do all of your spies masquerade as traders in alien space?"

"No, but trading and journalism are the best cover stories. We used to lose half of our recruits to the Galactic Free Press after a few years, so we started training reporters for them, and now the traffic flows both ways. The trainees you'll see today are journalists, so they don't get the extra trading classes."

The sound of clashing steel caught Kevin's attention, and he turned to watch two figures exchanging a flurry of attacks and parries with training foils. "Isn't that Clive's daughter?" he asked. "She can't be old enough to be training as an agent."

"Vivian has started coming in to fence with Judith when Samuel is at his new lost-and-found job," Thomas explained. "She has tremendous footwork thanks to her dance training, but she hasn't finished growing, and you can't teach reach. Come along," he added, as Kevin lingered to watch the contrast between the balletic movements of the young girl versus the energetic style of the athletic woman. "The Galactic Free Press brought in two of their reporters who were kidnapped by pirates to participate in the public hearing, and Clive thought you'd like to meet one of them."

"Here?"

"Chance uses holographic role playing to walk the journalism trainees through badly conceived attempts to get a scoop. Everybody's favorite is the one where Katya, who you'll be seeing in a minute, tells some Horten pirates that the Free Press has deep pockets, and that she wants to embed with their crew. She's a good sport for showing up and talking about it."

A group of around two dozen journalists of various ages stood gathered in front of the small platform where the holographic training sessions were conducted. Chance was standing on the stage chatting with a woman whose long black hair was tied back in a ponytail. The moment the artificial person saw that Thomas and Kevin had arrived, she launched into her introduction.

"So, everybody. This is Katya Wysecki, who was held hostage by pirates for two cycles before your employer received an invoice from the Tharks and was able to ransom her. Yes?" Chance asked, pointing at a middle-aged man who raised his hand.

"What do the Tharks have to do with it? I thought most of the pirates were Hortens."

"The Tharks handle anonymous monetary transactions for all species, on and off the tunnel network," Chance replied. "There was a delay in getting the demand for payment routed because the pirates communicate through couriers, and apparently they tried to negotiate the Tharks down on their fee."

"Leading to this," Katya interjected, turning her back to the audience and pulling her T-shirt up over her head without removing it. Her skin was richly tattooed with a scene of horses racing across a green plain. After giving the trainees a few seconds to gawk, she pulled the shirt back down and turned to face them again.

"They tortured you with tattoo work?" a young woman asked.

"I got bored as a hostage so I volunteered to help the crew's tattoo artist. That was how she paid me."

"Follow-up question," the same young reporter said. "Other than the boredom, you weren't, uh, abused in any way?"

"You mean aside from losing my freedom and being forced to subsist on a synthesized Vergallian vegan diet, which was the only food they could manage that wouldn't kill me? Keep in mind that the pirates kidnapped me because I was naïve enough to tell them that I worked for people with money. I spent the whole time on the one ship, and they didn't take any other captives, but they were open enough with their stories that I came to understand that my situation wasn't the norm. When pirates capture ships in space, they treat the survivors like slaves if they aren't from a local advanced species."

"Now I'm getting confused." This remark came from the same man who had asked the question about Thark involvement in the ransom. "The pirates play favorites depending on who they capture?"

"I don't want to give you the impression that I'm sympathetic to the pirates, but they're stuck in a delicate balancing act," Katya replied. "They don't have the military might to stand against the fleets of any of the advanced species, and it turns out that they can go broke paying reparations if they happen to attack the wrong ship. Pirates have no fear of humans, of course, but when it comes to attacking the shipping interests of other tunnel network members, they have to be very careful. Sticking with small traders that will surrender without a fight lets them minimize casualties."

"But what about all of the piracy stories on the Grenouthian news?" the same trainee protested. "They always have immersive footage of pitched battles."

"If you pay close attention, you'll see that most of those incidents take place in other parts of the galaxy, and the bunnies just license the imagery," Chance informed him. "You also have to differentiate between organized piracy, which you can think of as a multispecies crime syndicate, and rogue pirates. It's the rogues who are the most dangerous, but they never last for long since everybody is gunning for them, including the conventional pirates."

"How about talking a little about how you fell into captivity, Katya?" Thomas called out from the back of the audience where he stood with Kevin.

"Right. So I was going to be the first human reporter to embed with a pirate crew and write a story from the inside. I know, I know," she said, anticipating the reaction of the trainees and not pausing for questions. "I was caught up in a silly competition with a couple of other journalists, and I was even hoping I might capture some video with my implant that I could sell for cash to the Grenouthians."

"Is that allowed?" somebody called out.

"You're supposed to check with your editor first, but some reporters do it on the sly. The paper rarely runs video."

"Why not?" the same person asked.

"Our owner wants the focus to remain on the stories. The managing editor also said something about bandwidth costs and a special deal they have with the Stryx. Now where was I?"

"About to be kidnapped," Chance reminded her.

"Oh, yeah. So when I got out to the frontier, I started going around to shady looking Hortens and asking if anybody knew of a pirate crew willing to host a journalist. I finally found a contact who arranged for me to meet with some pirates in a bar, though I learned later that he basically sold me to them."

"But I heard that pirates honor their contracts," protested a young journalist with a number of visible tattoos.

"We didn't exactly make one," Katya admitted. "I know, I know. I'm lucky that the paper didn't tell the pirates to just keep me, though the articles I eventually wrote about my experience were so popular that I got a book offer out of it. Anyway, I boarded that pirate ship of my own free will, and I didn't even figure out I was a hostage until we visited an orbital and they wouldn't let me disembark to take a look around."

"Tell them what you do now," Chance suggested.

"So after subsisting on synthesized Vergallian grains and vegetables for over a hundred days, I really got into eating after I was ransomed. These days I'm the roving food and lifestyle editor. My mailbox at the paper is

157

'Katya,' so drop me a note if you come across any interesting recipes or alien foods during your travels that we can tolerate. If the paper hasn't run it before, you can write it up, and I'll make sure it gets counted towards your quota."

The trainees applauded politely as Katya stepped off the stage. Chance began passing out scripts to the class, and called up a hologram of a different kidnapping for role-playing. The ex-hostage made her way to where Thomas and Kevin were waiting.

"Katya Wysecki, this is Kevin Crick. Kevin is the young man who recently escaped from a pirate stronghold by stealing an old Verlock trader out of their trophy yard and activating the emergency retrieval network device."

"Pleased to meet you," Katya said, shaking hands enthusiastically. "What did you eat while you were in captivity?"

"Same as I always do," Kevin replied. "My trader was unarmed, so there wasn't any damage when they captured me. I had my standard three months of dehydrated and canned rations, plus a good part of my cargo. The two people I later escaped with had also been captured without a fight, and they were on an extended survey mission, so they had plenty of food of their own. I suppose we would have run out eventually if we hadn't gotten away, but I didn't really think that far ahead."

"Couldn't you arrange for ransom?"

"Nobody to pay it in my case. Molly, the scientist who was finishing a research contract after her husband died suddenly, said the pirates were trying to contact the consortium of Earth universities that paid for her research to demand a ransom. She knew that it would never get out of committee."

"That sucks," Katya said sympathetically. "Hey. Do you want to get something to eat?"

"Jeeves arrived during the presentation," Thomas informed the young man.

"I'm sorry, but I've got to get back to work," Kevin said. "Maybe another time."

"I'll probably see you at the hearing," Katya replied, and turned to the artificial person. "I don't suppose you know any good restaurants on this station?"

Kevin made his way back to the old campground section of Mac's Bones which now contained a dozen small ships towed back from the anniversary present lot. He glanced over at the fencing area, and saw Vivian standing on guard, while Judith rubbed her wrist and bent to pick up her foil. By the time he reached the Grenouthian lifeboat, it was surrounded by a faint haze and a smell like burnt hair. Joe was shaking his head at the Stryx in disgust.

"I didn't say I had ever worked one before," Jeeves protested. "I said that the theoretical underpinnings were simple enough. Nobody is good at everything."

"I still don't get why the bunnies would install a plasma harp in a lifeboat," Paul said. "There's barely room for two full-grown Grenouthians in emergency stasis pods, though they must have ripped those out for salvage before abandoning the boat in Gryph's long-term lot."

"What's a plasma harp?" Kevin asked.

"Jeeves claims that the bunnies get a bit panicky if they're stuck in enclosed spaces without two exits. I'd always wondered why they didn't have many small trading vessels. He said they use the harp to calm their nerves somehow."

159

"I just want to know how long that stink is going to last," Joe grumbled. "This lifeboat is a definite scrapper, so I want to finish stripping it before we start building a raft."

"A raft?" Kevin moved his hands about like he was putting together an invisible construct, an unconscious technique that helped him with spatial thinking. "Like a bunch of junked ships tied together floating through space?"

"We're going to have so much scrap metal by the time we work through all of Paul's ships that we'll get the best price by selling direct to one of the orbitals on the network," Joe replied. "Gryph can push it into the tunnel for a percentage. Less than it would cost in fuel to do it any other way."

"Why don't we take a look at that Sharf ship you liked while Jeeves is here?" Paul suggested to Kevin. "He should be able to tell us whether you'll need a new core before we start stripping down the old one."

"I haven't even put in a week's work yet and you're already trying to get rid of me?" Kevin joked half-seriously. "Am I that bad of a mechanic?"

"I'm a pushy salesman trying to close a deal," Paul responded. "Core issues aside, if you can get it space worthy in six months of working in your free time, you're a better wrench than either of us."

"You're speaking of the Sharf four-man scout that has been reconfigured as a trader, I assume," Jeeves said. "I can smell a minute gamma leak from here, which means the seals have held containment or there wouldn't be anything left to escape. Let's have a look."

The Stryx led the way to the scout ship, which was originally designed for speed and survivability rather than cargo capacity. Somebody had modified it by welding four large cargo carriers to the hull, obliterating its graceful lines. Jeeves floated through the open hatch of the technical deck and headed straight for the core, with the humans right behind him.

"Last owner shut it down properly, I'll give her that," the Stryx commented, circling the heart of the ship's power system. "Most trader captains leave them on standby, but after a few hundred years, there's nothing left to revive. This core hasn't been hot for over two thousand years, but I see no reason it shouldn't outlast you with a little bit of tuning."

"Why would anybody abandon a ship like this?" Kevin asked. "I know it's not beautiful and there's a limited market for mod-jobs, but if the control systems are as good as the core, it's got to be worth a hundred and fifty thousand, at least."

"Gryph informs me that at the time the last owner retired to Union Station, there was a glut of used Sharf traders on the market due to a new model being released. The owner still had a positive cash balance at the time of her death, and since there were no named heirs, it went to paying parking fees until the account was exhausted a few hundred years ago. Judging by the shape it's in, the Kurda was certainly fond of her ship."

"Kurda? I don't think I've ever come across that species," Joe said.

"There were a pair of them at your wife's ball, but they were wearing environmental suits, so there wasn't much to see. They do metabolize oxygen, but their air mix is too different from what you breathe to get by on nose filters. The Kurdas share a couple of harsh worlds with the Verlocks, as both species have a high tolerance for sulfuric acid in the air."

161

"So I'll have to swap out the atmospheric recycling system," Kevin concluded. "As long as the core is good, I can run some grow lights and add a garden to freshen up the air in the extra cabin space. I learned that from my mom."

"You're going to have to start scavenging for Zero-G exercise equipment wherever you can find it," Paul reminded him. "Come on. Let's go see if that stink has dispersed yet."

"You're not bringing in ships as fast as I thought you would," Jeeves commented.

"We don't see the point of filling the hold with unknowns until we sort out the ones we've already brought back," Paul said. "Besides, Joe doesn't want EarthCent Intelligence to think that we're pushing them out. There's actually plenty of room for everybody as long as we keep removing the hulks to build the raft in space."

"Just let me know if you want a hand selecting ships to bring in," the Stryx said. "I have a good nose for value, and I could save you some flight time on the Nova by dragging one or two in myself. I can do it without attachments these days."

"I remember when we were kids and all you did was complain about Libby making you study multiverse math," Paul reminded his friend. "Sounds like it's finally coming in handy."

"Math always comes in handy eventually," Jeeves replied.

Fourteen

Donna stuck her head through the door of Kelly's office and announced loudly, "Ambassador Srythlan to see you."

The EarthCent ambassador came awake with a start and bounded from her chair. Something the previous night had triggered the puppies to engage in a contest over who could produce the longest howl. Then Beowulf had joined in, and Joe had been forced to banish all three dogs from the ice harvester for the rest of the night, which only made them howl louder. Kelly ended up asking Libby to pipe in loud ocean sounds to cover up the racket, but her sleep had been disturbed by dreams about piratical canines insisting on their rights.

"Ambassador McAllister," Srythlan pronounced slowly. "I hope you don't mind my dropping by unannounced."

"Not at all, Srythlan. You're welcome anytime. Donna made arrangements for me to visit you at the Verlock embassy tomorrow, but perhaps your secretary didn't mention it."

"It is why I came," the Verlock said, moving slowly towards the chair in front of the ambassador's display desk. "I didn't want you to have to carry this back from my embassy." Srythlan deposited a dictionary-sized object wrapped in fine cloth on Kelly's desk. "I was coming out for the committee meeting at the Dollnick embassy in any case and I thought we might go together."

"Certainly, though that's not for another half an hour," Kelly replied. Then she realized that it must have taken the Verlock ambassador twenty minutes just to shuffle to her door from the lift tube, and that they would have to leave fairly soon to be on time for the meeting. "Is there any chance that this," she indicated the mystery package with a nod, "has something to do with the review?"

"You remain as perceptive as ever." Srythlan settled ponderously into the carbon fiber chair that groaned under his weight and began patting his own knee to speed up his speaking cadence from glacial to merely crawling "Our historical records indicate that you are required by the Stryx to solicit constructive criticism of your species from current tunnel network members."

"Yes," Kelly acknowledged with a grimace. "It's been...informative."

"I can sum up the Verlock view in just four words."

"We speak too fast? We move too fast? We aren't sufficiently thoughtful?" the EarthCent ambassador guessed in rapid succession, since they were operating under a time constraint.

"You are poorly educated," Srythlan continued, "especially in mathematics. It saddens me that we cannot discuss a wide variety of topics critical to the well-being of the galaxy due to your limited understanding of the underlying fundamentals."

"I know I only finished a year of university before I was recruited by the Stryx for EarthCent, but I'm pretty good at percentages."

The Verlock leaned forward and began deliberately unwrapping the package as he spoke. "My great-great-granddaughter, Rilrythe, is taking Alien Maths as a third year elective, and she chose to write her term paper on

164

Humans. I have spoken to her about your people at length, and she thought I would be interested in this primer she obtained at some trouble."

"Handbook of Mathematical Functions," Kelly read out the title, "Abramowitz and Stegun." She opened the heavy tome to the table of contents and gaped. "Are you sure that Rilrythe is only in her third year of university?"

"Her third year of schooling. She still watches 'Let's Make Friends' after doing her homework."

"Srythlan, I've never even heard of most of these things. Confluent Hypergeometric Functions? Combinatorial Analysis?" She spun the book around and tapped her finger on an upside-down entry, "Elementary Transcendental Functions? Anybody who puts the word 'Elementary,' in front of 'Transcendental Functions,' is either nutty or writing for an advanced audience. I'll bet that this book was intended as a reference for scientists and mathematicians."

"Are you sure? Rilrythe's term paper posited that it was an early Human attempt at an educational children's picture book. I perused the contents using a linear translator, and although the approach is often flawed, the text offers several novel ways to perform computations that produce correct answers within limited domains. I'm sure if you just worked with it a little each day, you'd find yourself caught up in the beauty." Srythlan flipped the book open at random, and triumphantly declared, "There. Aren't the illustrations lovely?"

Kelly stared at a representation of the contour lines for the modulus and phase of the Hankel Function and felt herself growing dizzy. Fortunately, Donna entered the office, and said, "I think you and Ambassador Srythlan need to get going if you're going to make the Dollnick embassy on time."

"Thank you, Donna. And thank you for the criticism and the gift, Srythlan. I'll give it my best shot."

"That's all that any of us can do," the Verlock replied philosophically. He rose to his feet and began shuffling towards the door. "Have your people been making any progress on the piracy issue?"

"You mean our intelligence people?" Kelly asked. Srythlan nodded in the affirmative. "I'm afraid our knowledge of piracy is limited to what we've learned from the humans who were captured by pirates and later ransomed or escaped, including Clive's sister. They'll be talking at the public hearing next week."

"Hmm. I've been briefed by our own intelligence people and they suggested a working relationship between the Humans of a colony world named 'Bits' and the pirates in that region. Nothing that rises to the level of strategic cooperation, but pirates depend on tolerance when it comes to finding markets for stolen goods."

"From what Paul told me about that place, it's basically a geek world peopled by programmers. They make a living by doing contract work for the highest bidder and creating their own games. Now that I think of it, he may have mentioned that they barter with pirates for alien military hardware that they can use to model new weapons."

"Here's what I heard," Srythlan said, and for the next fifteen minutes, managed about one word per step as they made their way to the lift tube, and then to the Dollnick embassy. "...So while nobody will accuse you of being in collusion with the pirates, it would be wise not to portray yourselves as completely innocent bystanders."

166

"Thank you," Kelly said again, as much because the Verlock ambassador had reached the end of his discourse as for the information imparted. "It looks like we're a bit early."

"Early is on time," the Dollnick ambassador greeted the new arrivals. He ushered them into the meeting room, which was already populated with most of the oxygen-breathing ambassadors. "I'm asking all of the participants today to acknowledge that I have not accepted chairmanship of this committee and that I am hosting this meeting purely as a matter of convenience to myself."

"If that's what you say, Crute," Kelly responded.

Srythlan waved a hand dismissively at the Dollnick, and the Grenouthian ambassador, who had arrived right behind them, said, "Live with it, Crute. It's your turn in the burrow."

"What does that mean?" Kelly subvoced Libby.

"You don't want to know," the Stryx librarian replied.

"Good, the catering is here," Czeros spoke up from the end of the table as a Gem entered the room. "Hey, there. Where's the food?"

"Are you addressing me, Ambassador?" the clone responded coldly. "I do not find your stereotype of my species as low-level service workers to be amusing."

"Ambassador Gem," the Crute greeted her. "Congratulations on your new appointment and thank you for responding to my invitation. There's an opening for committee chair if you're interested."

"Fat chance," the clone responded, taking the empty seat on Kelly's left. "Speaking of catering, where is it?"

"Ah, yes. About that," the Dollnick ambassador mumbled, looking a bit embarrassed. "I'm sure that some of you noticed that none of my staff are present today, and…"

"Are you pulling another 'Princely Fast Day' on us, Crute?" Bork demanded.

"In commemoration of the failed attempt to create a megastructure around the dwarf star Dinkel Three," the Dollnick ambassador explained. "A terrible loss of life and construction equipment."

"But you're the one who set the date for this meeting," Czeros objected.

"The fast day is why I had an opening in my schedule," Crute explained, spreading all four of his arms in a gesture of innocence.

"He's fasting so we don't get any food?" the Gem ambassador asked incredulously. "The only reason I accepted this job was because I wanted to feel what it would be like to have somebody to wait on me for a change."

"In honor of our Dollnick colleague's sacrifice in hosting this meeting on a day of mourning, I motion he be appointed permanent chair of this committee," Czeros suggested vindictively.

"Second the motion," the Gem affirmed without hesitation.

"Third," Ortha spoke at almost the same instant.

"All in favor?" Czeros raised his hand in answer to his own query, and every other two-armed ambassador present did the same.

"It's not too late to order out," Crute offered desperately, but he was met with stony silence. The giant Dollnick scowled at the others, then resignedly activated the boost mechanism on his chair, raising it above the level of the others in a token of his accepting the chairmanship. "I call this meeting of the latest committee foisted upon us by the Stryx to order. Has anybody made progress in determining what the lords of the tunnel network really want from us this time?"

"Our archivist has unearthed two previous demands to curtail piracy," the Grenouthian announced. "In the first instance, an immediate reduction of fifty percent in pirate vessels and a cap on recruitment at the subsequent replacement level was deemed sufficient. All of the tunnel network members kicked in for severance packages, and the species most involved," here the bunny paused and glanced at Czeros, "arranged for pensions for the elder members of their species who were thrown out of work."

"Don't know what you're on about," the Frunge ambassador mumbled, looking down at his hands.

"The prior intervention, taking place some two million years ago, involved an enterprising prince of the four-armed variety, who brought the same organizational talents to freebooting as his species currently applies to large engineering projects," the Grenouthian continued. "A ninety percent reduction in criminal activity was recorded when the Dollnick portion of the pirate forces accepted incentives to enter the space construction subcontracting business. I believe Prince Kuerda traces his family back to the Pirate Prince."

"The same Kuerda who won the contract for terraforming Venus?" Kelly asked.

Crute shrugged. "Ancient history."

"Our own archives include mention of a prior intervention, dating back some four million years," the Verlock ambassador added. "It seems that there was a fleet of Grenouthian…"

"I think we've spent enough time discussing precedents," the Grenouthian ambassador interrupted his slow-spoken colleague. "In both instances, the Stryx settled for a substantial reduction in the baseline level of piracy, coupled with a mechanism to prevent it from springing right back. In one case, the follow-up involved buying off a part of the pirate population, in the other, steering the pirates into gainful employment. Perhaps our Horten colleague has some ideas on this subject?"

Ortha was apparently prepared for this question because he immediately launched into his response. "I've opened a channel of communications with the primary piracy organization, and some of you have already met the advocate they retained to represent their side at the upcoming public hearing. The pirates are open to negotiating a reduction in activity..."

"And not getting wiped out," Abeva inserted when Ortha paused for effect.

"But they demand that certain traditional prerogatives be respected. They also wish the record to show the role they have played in absorbing refugees from authoritarian regimes, such as the recent influx from the collapsing Gem Empire, and their restraint in dealing with the territorial incursions of less advanced species who don't know any better," the Horten ambassador concluded, making a casual hand motion that seemed to indicate the EarthCent ambassador.

"Let's keep this short so those of us who aren't fasting can get something to eat," Bork suggested. "We're talking about a reduction of between fifty to seventy percent in organized activity, along with a plausible reemployment program for the pirates who draw the short straw."

"All of my sisters are welcome to return home, but if there is to be a compensation package, I will advise them to hold out for whatever their compatriots receive," the Gem ambassador announced. "It's only fair."

"If Ambassador Ortha can provide me with the current employment rolls for the pirates, showing ranks and time of service, I shall have my staff prepare an array of options, along with the associated costs," Srythlan offered.

"Did we just reach some sort of agreement?" Kelly asked. "What about the hearings? We have several victims of piracy waiting to testify."

"I see no reason to cancel the hearings," Crute said, taking his revenge on the Horten ambassador for participating in the motion to make the Dollnick accept the committee chairmanship. "Due to ongoing time constraints, I decree that our next gathering take place concurrently with the previously scheduled meeting to discuss our recommendation to the Stryx on the Human review issue. I'm sure the EarthCent ambassador won't mind stepping out in the corridor at the appropriate time."

"When is that?" Kelly asked, but she was drowned out by the scraping of chairs, as the diplomats who had forgone eating in anticipation of a free meal made a run for the door. A moment later she found herself alone with Ambassador Crute and the slow-moving Verlock, who would need a couple of minutes to make his way out of the embassy. "I didn't even know you were all meeting to discuss your recommendations to the Stryx," she tried again.

"I'll have my secretary send the information to your embassy after the fast," the Dollnick responded. His body language implied that discussing such mundane details was below him. "It's bad enough that the Stryx insisted I make room for you on my schedule tomorrow. I'll be missing part of a presentation on resort planet financing for the sake of your little consciousness-raising session."

"Why not do it right now?" Kelly offered.

Crute glanced at the Verlock ambassador, who had just reached the end of the table and was shuffling slowly towards the door, after which there was still a corridor and a lobby to traverse before the embassy could be locked up. "Very well," the Dollnick agreed, and returned to his seat. "The station librarian informs me that I'm…"

"To offer constructive criticism," Kelly interjected, hoping to steer his remarks away from outright insults. "I thought you might want to discuss human contract laborers on Dollnick worlds, since that's far and away the most common point of contact between our species."

"Are you sure you require my presence to solicit my views?" Crute asked sarcastically. "You seem to be quite capable of conducting both sides of the conversation."

"Sorry, that's just me. I hope you don't hold it against humanity. So what do the Dollnicks really think of us?"

Crute hesitated uncharacteristically and mumbled something to himself before answering. "The problem is your conversational style. Humans display a need to talk even when they have nothing of value to add to the discussion. You confuse asking questions with listening, and you don't differentiate between making thoughtless suggestions and genuine contributions. Prince Kuerda once told me that the terraforming workers on one of his projects are always…"

"Trying to negotiate better terms for an iron-clad contract they've already signed?" Kelly interrupted, and then shrank as the giant ambassador glowered at her. "I'm sorry. I was told that Dollnicks find things like that amusing."

"May I continue?" Crute inquired acerbically. "Prince Kuerda complains that Human workers are always finishing the sentences of their supervisors, and as with your own recent transgressions, they're always wrong! Do you have any idea how frustrating it is for a construction engineer to be bothered throughout the day with suggestions for changing standard practices that have been tweaked over millions of cycles, and then interrupted with wild guesses every time he tries to explain?"

"It can't be very..."

"Dollnick managers are chosen for their willingness to listen to feedback from work crews to ensure that the job progresses smoothly and on schedule," Crute talked over her. "They come up through the ranks and know their jobs inside out. Prince Kuerda has determined that the Dollnicks who work in direct contact with Humans need special training NOT to take the suggestions of their crews seriously. He spoke of a veteran rigging supervisor who had a nervous breakdown after being forced to explain the principle of space elevator operation over and over again to workers who couldn't or wouldn't understand what holds the cable taut!"

"I imagine that..."

"I'm not angry about your ignorance," the Dollnick ambassador continued, the volume of his speech becoming louder and louder. "I'm angry that you refuse to keep it to yourself. Humans, I mean," he concluded, his voice falling back from the shrill whistle that Kelly's implant had been unable to fully cancel out with the simultaneous translation.

The EarthCent ambassador waited until she was sure Crute had completed his rant before venturing, "So we talk too much when we should be listening, and we interrupt?"

"There is one other thing—but no, I'd rather not mention it."

"Thank you for the criticism, Ambassador. Though I might say in our defense that you did accept my suggestion to have this little chat now, rather than waiting for tomorrow," Kelly pointed out as she rose to her feet.

"THAT'S IT!" the Dollnick trilled. "In the one-in-a-thousand case that your species actually gets something right, you insist on trumpeting the fact like you've come up with a solution for damping down unstable stars. I told you so, I told you so," he cried in imitation, and then, crossing his lower set of arms to make a pillow for his head on the conference table, he placed the hands from his upper set of arms over his ears.

Kelly took the clue and left the room, wondering if fasting made the giant alien cranky.

Fifteen

"Welcome to our anniversary party," Aisha greeted the Grenouthian producer of her show. She was dressed in her best sari, and with Dorothy's help, had attired Paul in a fashionable suit. "I'm counting on you to get the rest of the production crew to mingle," she added, pointing towards the knot of giant bunnies standing apart from the rest of the guests and drinking specially prepared cocktails through novelty straws. "Especially when the dancing starts."

"I'll see if anything can be done," the producer replied noncommittally. He nodded to Paul and hopped off towards the other Grenouthians.

"Mrs. McAllister, Mr. McAllister," the Horten ambassador greeted the hosts formally. "Allow me to introduce Advocate Jursha, who is staying with my family."

"I am honored to meet the most famous Human in the galaxy," Jursha stated, making a formal bow. "I don't usually go about crashing parties, but when Ortha told me that his son's band was playing, I couldn't resist. I understand that the young man has put aside his awful caterwauling style and thuggish presentation to become one of the most in-demand crooners on the station."

"Weddings, anniversaries, and coming-of-age ceremonies," the Horten ambassador said. "I wish I had thought

175

of cutting off his allowance years ago, but better late than never."

"I'm just glad he could fit us into his schedule," Aisha told the proud father. "Fortunately, my sister-in-law knows your son from somewhere and was able to convince him."

"Wait until you see the band's catering bill," Paul said to his wife after the Hortens moved past. "Clive, Blythe. Welcome to our anniversary party. Samuel is working the grill with Joe, Vivian, but we're counting on the two of you to help get the dancing started. You too, Jonah."

After the expanded Oxford clan chorused their "Happy Anniversary" greetings, Blythe added, "I don't think you've been introduced to Molly and Nigel, Clive's sister and nephew."

"Not yet, but Kevin has told us all about you," Aisha replied, leaning forward and giving Molly a hug. "He's working with my husband and he's here practically all the time now." She lowered her voice and glanced around before adding, "He and Dorothy seem to be hitting it off."

"Then we should all take up a collection to persuade him to stick around," Clive observed, before urging his family forward. "Let's go. We're holding up the line."

Aisha spent the next ten minutes greeting dozens of young aliens who were current and former cast members of her show, most of whom were accompanied by parents. The fact that they had all showed up at the same time made her suspicious that they had coordinated their arrivals because they were uncomfortable about attending a human celebration. Aisha had hired the same Gem catering outfit that the Grenouthians used for cast parties, so she was confident that at least the guests wouldn't go hungry.

176

After the anniversary couple greeted the last of the show-related aliens, Woojin stepped forward with the Farling doctor by his side. "Lynx made me come because she's tired of watching me watch her," he explained. "I didn't want to leave her alone, but she insisted that nothing is going to happen for another four days."

"Plus nine hours and thirteen minutes," the giant beetle said. "Mr. Lynx refused to leave her until I arrived to confirm the obvious, though I fear I am setting a bad precedent for doctors everywhere by making house calls. For you," he added, presenting the host of "Let's Make Friends" with a watch.

"What's this?" Aisha asked, even though she had heard all about the alien doctor's famous countdown watches.

"I checked with the Stryx librarian and I understand that a wristwatch is the appropriate gift for a fifteenth wedding anniversary," the alien beetle reassured her. "Sometimes a watch is just a watch."

After Woojin and the Farling continued on towards the grill, Paul asked his wife, "What time does it say?"

"It's not showing a time, it's counting down," Aisha replied in a whisper. "Ten months and two weeks."

"Why do I get the feeling that sometimes a watch is an advertisement," Paul said. He looked around for the doctor as he spoke, and was surprised to see his adopted daughter run up to the Farling and greet the alien familiarly. "Honey? Has Fenna been talking to you about the baby brother thing again lately?"

"Happy anniversary," Thomas and Chance declared together. The two artificial people were the last ones left in the reception line, and both were dressed to the nines in their tango togs.

"Thank you for coming," Aisha responded sincerely, though she was still trying to wrap her head around the Farling's gift. "We're counting on you guys to help the kids get the dancing started. You know what these mixed species crowds with children are like."

"Looks like they'll be busy demolishing the food for a while yet," Chance said. "Would you mind if I asked the band to play a little tango? I heard them at a wedding for one of our trainees last month and they're surprisingly good at cross-species music."

"Hortens have perfect memories for musical scores, but very few of them can sing," Thomas contributed. "Their ambassador's son is an exception."

"I think that would be lovely," Aisha said, acquiescing to Chance's request. She glanced again towards the entrance of Mac's Bones to make sure that she wasn't turning her back on any late-arriving guests, and then headed with Paul towards the food tables. The pair broke up when Aisha stopped at the vegetarian spread and her husband continued on to the grill.

Standing behind the grill line, Vivian was toasting hamburger rolls while explaining to Samuel that she was really older than him because girls mature faster than boys. "Being female is worth at least three years, so you're almost a year behind me."

"I'm two years older than you," Samuel insisted. "I turned fifteen a couple months ago and you just turned thirteen. The Vergallians say…"

"The Vergallians aren't here," she cut him off abruptly. "Are we done, Mr. McAllister?"

"These two are for you," Joe said, sliding a medium burger onto a toasted roll for each of the kids, and a patty directly onto his foster son's plate. "Paul is off of bread until he gets rid of that spare tire. Thank you both for the help."

"I haven't let my belt out in years," Paul objected loudly, and then asked under his breath, "Have you heard from Jeeves?"

"Everything is set and he'll check with you before popping the bay doors."

"Great. Are you shutting down the grill line already?"

"I wasn't figuring on the Frunge bypassing the Gem caterers and practically cleaning me out of raw meat," Joe explained. "It's a good thing they all came late or some of your friends would have gone hungry. I am kind of surprised to see the adults who accompanied Aisha's cast members are ordering drinks like it's the end of prohibition."

"She said that a lot of them don't have any experience with humans outside of their kids being on the show. They're probably nervous about us doing weird human stuff."

"Get some potato salad to go with that burger, but don't take too long eating or Jeeves will have time to start improvising. I don't think you want that."

"Good point," Paul acknowledged. He took his plate over to where Aisha sat at a table of mixed aliens and was working to put them at ease.

Libby subtly altered the lighting in Mac's Bones so that it seemed as if the couple on the dance floor had appeared out of nowhere when the Horten band struck up a tango. Within moments, everybody's eyes were fixed on the artificial people. Thomas and Chance moved with such extraordinary grace and speed that anybody who hadn't witnessed a professional Argentine tango could be forgiven for thinking that the couple's legs were in danger of becoming hopelessly intertwined in a knot.

Paul massaged the skin under his chin between his thumb and forefinger as if he were regretting a bad shave, but in reality he was trying to cover up subvocing to Jeeves. "We're all eating. Yes, Aisha asked where you were, but I don't think she suspects anything. Thomas and Chance have everybody mesmerized, so now is perfect."

The large bay doors of Mac's Bones silently slid open, and the triple-decker habitat painted to match the ice harvester slipped through the atmosphere retention field, suspended by Jeeves. Paul and Joe were the only ones who witnessed the Stryx deftly guiding the boxy structure around the overhead lights so as not to cast shadows. Joe had cleaned up an area of deck next to the ice harvester, joking that he wanted to raise chickens in his retirement, and Jeeves eased the renovated alien habitat into position.

When the tango came to an end, Paul touched his wife lightly on the shoulder and whispered, "Happy Anniversary."

Aisha smiled as she set down her spoon and turned toward her husband. Her eyes went wide and there were gasps from the surprised guests as Libby dramatically brought up the lights on the new dwelling. It seemed to have appeared out of nowhere as if conjured by magic.

"Paul! Is that what I think it is?"

"It's from the auction lot you gave me, though I had the Dollnicks a few bays over spruce it up for us. It might be a few days before Joe and I can get the plumbing hooked up, but it's all freshly painted with that Cappuccino White you said you like, and Dorothy made the curtains. I know you've always wanted a meatless kitchen, and living next door is a way of having our own home without losing out on the babysitting. It's just empty rooms now, but you can furnish it any way you want—any way you and Fenna want."

"It's beautiful," Aisha breathed, struggling to take in the giant blue ribbon, which included a bow right over the front entrance.

The guests all began clapping as if the Grenouthians had lit up an "applause" sign, and taking Fenna between them, Paul and Aisha approached their new house.

"Nice hutch," the producer of "Let's Make Friends" called to his star as the humans passed the Grenouthian table.

"Does this mean they're moving out?" Kelly asked Joe. "Nobody ever tells me anything."

"I was worried you might explode if you had to keep a secret for two weeks," her husband joked. "Besides, you're so wound up in the review business that I doubt it would have registered. Now you'll have two more rooms available for bringing home strays to run off with Dorothy's boyfriends."

The Horten musicians struck up a techno-waltz, the small-band substitute for ballroom dancing, and this time Samuel and Vivian put on an exhibition for the guests. A few of the more adventurous humans joined in the next song, along with Thomas and Chance, but the aliens all sat on their hands and watched passively.

Dorothy approached the bandstand and motioned Mornich over. "Aisha put me in charge of the entertainment and she wants everybody to participate," she told the Horten. "I don't know anything about getting alien children to dance. I only go to parties with people our age."

"Your friends were too good," Mornich explained. "Humans don't care how they look after a few drinks, but most species hate to make fools out of themselves on the dance floor, especially in front of each other. They might have gotten over the two artificials doing the tango, that's specialist stuff that none of them have ever seen, but those kids dancing Vergallian style are intimidating."

"I'll get them to take a break," Dorothy promised. "My sister-in-law really wants the children from her cast to have a good time. Don't you have any standards for those coming-of-age parties you do that will get them all out on the dance floor?"

"Well, there's always the Stryx dance," Mornich said with a sigh. "I don't pull that one out unless I have to because the music is just dreadful and I get stuck leading it."

"Does the music get everybody to dance?"

"Like zombies under compulsion," the Horten replied with a barely restrained shudder. "As soon as I announce it, the parents will push their kids onto the dance floor, and then they'll follow themselves, like it's been pro-grammed into their genes. It almost scares me sometimes."

"Will humans be able to do it?"

"I don't know. Can you all count to four?"

"Let's put it in next. I'm afraid some of the kids might leave before Aisha even gets back from checking out her house."

Mornich nodded his assent and began making hand signals to the band members, who were winding down the current instrumental. Dorothy headed back to the twenty-something table and harvested Kevin.

"You're dancing in this next one," she told him. "It's make-or-break for the party."

"As long as you don't expect me to be any good," he replied, rising to his feet. "I've only danced with my sisters, and that was a long time ago."

"This should be perfect, then," Dorothy said as the music died out. "It's…"

"Time to do the Stryx dance," Mornich announced, walking out onto the dance floor with a large handheld microphone that was obviously designed to draw attention rather than for functionality. "Come on, parents. Get those kids on the floor."

The percussionist began playing a sort of an extended introduction in four/four time. As the Horten had predicted, every one of the aliens moved onto the dance floor, including the Grenouthian crew, whose whiskers twitched weirdly with the beat. Another member of the band began playing a lilting melody on a keyboard, and the dancers all formed up in a grid, as if the deck had been marked with crossing lines.

"Left foot," Mornich called, sliding out his left leg and touching the toe on the floor. He repeated the move twice with the beat and called, "Right foot."

"It's the Alley Cat," Kelly said to Joe, getting up from the table and pulling him to his feet. "Come on. Even we can do this."

"Left knee," the Horten cried, lifting his left knee twice in time with the keyboard notes, and then shifting to the right. "Clap and turn."

Over a hundred aliens, many of them wearing maniacal grins by this point, clapped simultaneously and jumped in the air, landing faced ninety degrees from their original position.

The keyboardist began replaying the exact same melody from the start, but the percussionist picked up the beat almost imperceptibly, and the dancers all worked their way successfully through three hundred and sixty degrees, including the slow-footed Verlocks.

"Arms!" Mornich commanded, and the sequence repeated, this time with the dancers moving their arms in time with their legs, and opening their hands at the end of each reach.

"This isn't that bad," Joe admitted, dancing never having been his thing. "Reminds me of kindergarten."

"Double," Mornich cried at the end of the second rotation. "Back and kick."

Kelly and Joe were both caught clapping and jumping when all of the aliens and most of the humans were instead extending a foot out behind them for two counts on each leg, and then kicking forward, doubling the length of the sequence. Meanwhile, the percussionist continued to slowly increase his beat, and the Verlocks began struggling to keep up.

"What are you doing?" the Horten ambassador called to Kelly as she tried to settle into the new regime. "You're out."

"What do you mean I'm out?"

"It's an elimination dance," Ortha said, lifting a knee high in perfect timing with the notes. "No mistakes allowed."

"Come on, Kel," Joe said, putting an arm around his wife's waist and leading her off the dance floor. "The kicking bit is dicey for my knees in any case."

"Opposing arm!" Mornich ordered as the round came to an end, and the dancers began doing the reach move with the arm opposite to the leg being moved. The tune repeated a little faster, and the older Verlocks shuffled off of the dance floor.

Kelly and Joe returned to their seats, where Dring was chatting with M793qK. The ambassador looked around and realized to her surprise that Thomas and Chance had also sat this one out. The artificial people, the Maker, and the Farling were the only ones in the hold who weren't at least bobbing their heads compulsively with the beat.

The beetle noticed the EarthCent ambassador observing him, and inquired, "Out already? Something wrong with your genetic programming? If you come into my shop I can take a look."

"What are you talking about?" Kelly demanded.

"He's just joking," Dring said, scowling at the Farling, who spread a number of his limbs in a mock sign of surrender. "There's nothing wrong with a little line dance competition from time to time."

"Double tap, triple clap" Mornich called, and the dancers began double tapping their toes at the end of each leg reach and triple clapping with each jump, a move that eliminated most of the remaining humans and older aliens.

"When does it end?" Kelly asked.

"That depends on the caller," Dring explained. "Since this isn't a competition and the crowd is mixed, I suspect he'll stop on the tenth round, depending on whether he feels the guests are sufficiently loosened up to keep on dancing."

A triple clap sounded from behind them, and Kelly turned to see that Paul and Aisha had returned from their tour of the remodeled habitat with their daughter and Jeeves. Fenna had started mimicking the moves of the dancers, while Aisha and Paul were bobbing their heads.

"Give up already?" Paul inquired.

"We got eliminated, it's not the same thing," Joe replied. "Did the Dollys finish everything on time?"

185

"It's wonderful," Aisha enthused, moving her hands unconsciously in time with the music. "The kitchen is gorgeous, and I've never seen such a large bathroom. Paul said that you've already fabricated stairways to weld in so we can get to the upper floors."

Beowulf, who along with the puppies had been watching the dancers, twisted his head towards the new arrivals and sniffed suspiciously. Then he went right up to Jeeves, his tail wagging like crazy, and thrust his nose against the Stryx's casing.

"The nose always knows," Jeeves said. He slid his pincer into a hidden slot and pulled out a well chewed boomerang toy. "I found this bouncing around Union Station's core while I was bringing your house over, and I recognized the bite marks."

Out on the dance floor, Mornich called, "Four-fifty," and with the next clap the dancers all tried to complete a full turn and a quarter as they jumped in the air. When the melody began to repeat, Samuel, Vivian, and Jonah were the only humans left in competition.

Sixteen

"It's in the Galaxy Room at the Empire Convention Center?" Kelly asked in surprise. "I thought it would be held in the Stryx meeting room, maybe with some immersive coverage."

"It's a public hearing," Libby explained. "We had planned on a smaller venue, but ticket sales went through the roof when the Hortens announced that Advocate Jursha would be representing the pirates."

"Representing them how? Is he going to claim that the people taken hostage were actually attacking the pirates or something? And what did you mean by ticket sales?" she added, when the middle part of the station librarian's reply sank in.

"Surely you don't begrudge Gryph earning back the fees he paid the Farling for the medical care given to Clive's long-lost relatives and the Crick boy."

"But the Verlocks were willing to pay for that," Kelly argued. "And you didn't answer my question about Jursha."

"That's because you changed the subject. Even though this is a hearing and not a trial, it wouldn't be fair to solicit just one side of the story."

"One side of the story? But you're the ones who told the rest of us to do something about the pirates or else."

"That was Jeeves, actually, and he might have expressed our views a little more forcefully than we intended. It's his first major diplomatic assignment, after all."

"So this Jursha guy is going to get up and say nice things about the pirates?"

"We try to accommodate the practices of member species in all official tunnel network business. I'm afraid that the Hortens conduct their legal system in the manner of a game, and Jursha is the reigning advocacy champion. If we hadn't set aside blocks of tickets for each species, the amphitheatre would have sold out to an all-Horten crowd. Of course, you have to prepare for scalping."

"Our witnesses are in danger of being assaulted?"

"Ticket scalping, not the frontier kind. There are several businesses on the station that specialize in purchasing and reselling reserved blocks of tickets for popular events."

"And you allow it?"

"Nobody is being forced to sell," Libby pointed out. "Our intention is to provide equal access to the public events we schedule, but attendance isn't compulsory, and there are plenty of profits for everybody to share around. You really should get going if you want to arrive early."

"Good grief," the ambassador said, rising from her desk and heading for the lift tube. "It's starting to sound like a circus."

When Kelly reached the Empire Convention Center, she found that the lift tube had brought her to the deck below the public entrances for the Galaxy Room. The ambassador hadn't been through the maze of tunnels and meeting rooms underneath the stadium seating for a number of years, and got herself hopelessly turned around several times before asking Libby for directions. When she finally emerged on the stage at the center of the amphitheatre, she found that chairs of the proper type for each of the oxygen-breathing tunnel network ambassadors were placed in an arc facing twin lecterns. Only one of the chairs was unoccupied.

"On time is late," the Grenouthian ambassador remarked loudly as the EarthCent ambassador passed him on the way to her seat.

Kelly checked her heads-up display and discovered that she had arrived just as the hearing was scheduled to start. The room was eerily quiet. She squinted against the lights to get an idea of the audience in attendance, and concluded that ticket holders were approximately eighty percent Hortens.

A moment later, at precisely the correct time, Crute rose and began to speak from where he stood. His voice was picked up and amplified for the audience by the array of directional pickups above the stage.

"Welcome to our public hearing assessing the impact of piracy on tunnel network members. The testimony will start with the presentation of four Human witnesses, as most of us believe that this disruption in the status quo is due to the Stryx's desire to protect their latest favored species." The Dollnick ambassador paused as thousands of Hortens stomped their feet and hissed. "The first witness is a young man who lost his ship to the pirates shortly after paying off the mortgage. He escaped from captivity by stealing a museum-quality Verlock trader with two Human accomplices and activating the obsolete VTGERN device. Kevin Crick, please take the stand."

Kevin walked from one of the tunnel openings under the stadium seating and approached the nearer lectern as Crute sat back down. Since the Dollnick had already introduced him, the young man launched directly into his testimony, starting with the day that he responded to a distress call from another human ship, only to find that it was a false signal sent out by a pirate squadron looking for easy prey. By the time he reached the end of his story, touching briefly on the radiation poisoning treatments, even a few of the Hortens in the crowd were looking sympathetic.

"We have heard the testimony of the first Human," Crute announced, not bothering to stand this time. "I now invite Advocate Jursha to cross-examine the witness."

"Cross-examine?" Kelly subvoced the station librarian.

"It's a Horten tradition," Libby replied.

Jursha strode up to the second lectern, looking exactly like an immersive star in a courtroom drama, and the audience burst into a roar of applause. The Horten smoothed a few imaginary wrinkles from his ten-thousand-cred suit, and made a little movement halfway between a wave and a salute to acknowledge the crowd, which responded with renewed enthusiasm. Then he turned to face Kevin with a friendly smile.

"Mr. Crick. I've been retained by the Free Republic to clarify their position vis-à-vis the allegations you have made today."

"It's all the truth," the young man asserted.

"I'm sure you believe that," the advocate replied evenly, "but as a point of order, I must ask that you speak only when addressed. I'm sure you appreciate that nobody interrupted your testimony."

Kevin shrugged and nodded.

"Thank you. I would like to start by asking you to put a monetary value on the ship and cargo you claim to have lost to my clients."

190

"Two hundred thousand creds for the ship, a used Sharf trader for which I had just paid off the mortgage. The cargo was primarily sporting equipment and processed foods, for which I paid twenty-three thousand two-hundred creds wholesale."

"Let's be generous and round up to a quarter million Stryx creds," the advocate offered. "Would that be fair compensation, including your time?"

"It's very generous, but…"

"No need to protest that it's more than you deserve," Jursha interrupted. "Now, if we can revisit one of the highlights of your testimony, you admit to having over-loaded the stasis field generator on your host's asteroid base, after which you absconded with an antique Verlock vessel. Can you describe the state of said stasis field generator the last time you saw it?"

"It was smoking, and I guess there were sparks shooting out of the vents."

"You guess there were sparks shooting out of the vents. Do you know how much a stasis field generator with that kind of coverage capacity costs?"

"A lot?" Kevin hazarded a guess.

"Over five million creds, and that's if you can get the Stryx to sell you the components," Jursha thundered. "Industrial stasis field generators are on the restricted list, and none of the local species have succeeded in duplicating the effect."

"The pirates probably stole it somewhere," Kevin objected.

"Immaterial! And what value would you put on the Verlock vessel?"

"Well, the Stryx accepted it in trade to pay for our rescue and…"

"You took a ship that did not belong to you and sold it?" Lorsha interjected.

"In a manner of speaking, maybe, but..."

"I think I've made my point about monetary damages, but my employers are willing to waive their rights in this case," the advocate continued, drawing a round of laughter and applause from the audience. "After all, we are all friends on the tunnel network, and I believe I saw you just the other evening doing the Stryx dance. Is that so?"

"I don't remember you, but I guess it's possible."

"May I ask the identity of the lovely young woman you were escorting?"

"I don't see why I should answer that."

"Then let me answer for you," Jursha said. "You were dancing with Dorothy McAllister, the daughter of the EarthCent Ambassador, who is the Human member of the committee responsible for this hearing!"

The audience exploded in another round of boot-stomping and hooting. Jursha inserted one hand in the breast of his suit, and began pacing around the lectern to make sure that the entire audience got a chance to see him from the front.

"I'm not here to make accusations about nepotism and insider dealing among Humans," the Horten continued. "My question for you is, do you love her?"

"Do I what?" Kevin stuttered, blushing beneath his radiation tan and looking around as if he expected support from some unseen ally.

"Although I don't pretend to be an expert in Human color changes, I believe 'Yes,' is written all over your face. My final question to you is, would have been dancing with the object of your affections if not for the intervention of my clients in your otherwise humdrum existence?"

192

Kevin gaped at the Horten advocate, at a complete loss for words.

"No further questions," Jursha declared to the thunderous applause from the packed amphitheatre.

Crute waited for Kevin to leave the lectern before calling out, "The next witness is one Katya Wysecki, an employee of the Galactic Free Press who was a guest of the Free Republic, I mean, pirates, while on a journalistic assignment. You may give your testimony, Ms. Wysecki."

"Guest?" Kelly demanded of the Stryx librarian over her implant. "Chastity had to pay a ransom to get her back!"

Libby didn't answer, and Katya took her place at the lectern. She repeated her story about trying to find a pirate crew that would accept an embedded reporter, only to find herself held hostage for ransom. Jursha could be seen nodding sympathetically as she spoke, and made no effort to dispute any of the darker incidents she reported.

"A disturbing tale of a life-altering experience," the Horten said when Katya reached the end of her testimony. "Does that sound familiar to you?"

"It's certainly a fair summary," the reporter replied, but then a strange look came over her face. "Isn't that the cover blurb from my pre-release book? I just got that myself."

"Your pre-release book," the Horten repeated. "Tell us honestly, now. Would you have landed a six-figure advance for a book deal if not for the time you spent with my clients?"

"That's blaming the victim!" Katya retorted, but nobody heard her words over the boot-stomping and whistling from the audience.

"And may I ask your current occupation?" Jursha continued as soon as the noise died down.

"I'm the roving food and lifestyle editor for the Galactic Free Press."

"Editor. So the time you spent with my clients led to a promotion and enhanced career opportunities?"

"You're twisting what happened," Katya objected, but if anybody could hear her over the renewed applause, they weren't buying it.

"In addition to the book contract and your promotion, didn't you take away something else from your time on the frontier?"

"An aversion to synthesized Vergallian vegan," she replied, drawing a few sympathetic chuckles from audience members who had spent time eating the galaxy's safest diet for humanoids.

"Are you sure there's nothing else you'd like to share with us?" Jursha insisted.

"I don't—do you mean my tattoo?" Katya asked.

"I'm told that a sixty-four color full-back tattoo in the Free Republic style takes many weeks to ink and would cost several thousand creds on this station."

"But that was in payment for the work I did."

"As a member of the ship's crew," Jursha insinuated.

"Yes, as a—no," Katya corrected herself, but it was too late, and the whole amphitheatre sounded with cries of admiration for the Horten advocate.

"No further questions," Jursha declared.

"This is a travesty," Kelly hissed at Crute, but the committee chairman waved her off with one of his lower arms while pointing at his own ear with the upper arm on the same side. After completing the subvoced conversation, he rose to speak.

"It appears that our third Human witness, a correspondent of the Galactic Free Press who stowed away on a

Free Republic vessel, is unwilling to face Advocate Jursha and has flown the proverbial coop." Deafening hoots and stomping from the Horten audience drowned out the Dollnick ambassador's next sentence, and he waited impatiently for the opportunity to continue. "The final witness is one Molly Blackthorne, who was carrying out an archeological survey contract with her son prior to joining, I mean, being taken by the Free, uh, pirates."

Molly emerged from the tunnel, stalked proudly to the lectern, and shot the Dollnick ambassador an angry look before commencing her testimony. She described the moment her ship was hit by a suppression field while in orbit over the ghost planet of Hevel Five, and the terror of having the outer hatch of the airlock forced open by pirates in armored spacesuits. When she concluded her testimony with how she awoke to seeing a giant beetle standing over her, and punched him with her good arm before learning that he was a doctor, the audience remained respectfully silent.

Jursha allowed a full minute to pass, his head bowed in sympathy. Then he touched a control on his lectern and a giant hologram of a spaceship appeared over the stage, rotating slowly through three hundred and sixty degrees. The advocate nodded his head in satisfaction, took hold of the lapels of his suit, and addressed Molly.

"Do you recognize the vessel in this hologram?"

"That's the Ivy League Explorer, the ship our sponsors provided my husband for the contract."

"And after your husband's unexpected demise, you decided to continue his work and complete the contract."

"I met my husband in graduate school where we were both studying archeology, and I also hold a doctoral degree in that field."

195

"And your only crew on this mission was your young son?"

"Yes, that's correct," Molly replied cautiously, unable to see where the advocate was leading her.

"May I assume that neither of you are experts in fusion cores or spaceship engineering in general."

"Yes, but I can recognize the ship. The name is painted on the stern."

"Prow," Jursha corrected her gently, and touched another control on the lectern. Something that looked like a circulatory system appeared in the hologram, thick lines pulsing with reds and blues, all connected to a wavering white blob on the technical deck. A sudden chorus of whispers rose from the audience, and the advocate allowed time for a full rotation of the hologram before asking, "Do you understand what is represented here?"

"It looks very familiar," Molly admitted. "I recall seeing something similar projected from the ship controller when we arrived at Hevel Five."

"What we are looking at is the critical systems failure warning which was downloaded from the Ivy League Explorer's ship controller. The yellow outline around the hologram indicates that the controller was instructed to suppress all warning messages short of impending catastrophic failure. May I ask if you know where the ship was purchased?"

"I went with my husband to look at it before we accepted the contract. There was a dealer in Earth orbit selling used Sharf vessels, and the university consortium had just bought it for the mission."

The Horten touched a control in his lectern again, and the hologram of the ship was replaced by an image of a handsome man who one might expect to see in an advertisement for corporate services.

"Do you recognize this individual?"

"He's the dealer who showed us the ship."

"The Human in question is currently serving a life sentence in an Earth penitentiary for knowingly selling defective spaceships purchased as scrap metal from a Sharf recycling facility. His offenses ranged from removing 'condemned' stickers to disabling error reporting functions on controllers. A number of buyers less fortunate than yourself have found their deaths in this evil man's merchandise."

A sound like heavy rain filled the room as the Hortens in the audience all tapped their heels to indicate a lucky escape.

"You're trying to claim that the pirates saved our lives?" Molly asked incredulously.

"There can be no doubt," the advocate asserted. "Your ship could not have broken orbit on its own, and the suppression field extended by my clients prevented an impending implosion." Jursha waved in acknowledgement of the loud round of applause, before adding for Molly's benefit, "The data I just presented was reviewed and approved by the Stryx. There's just one more line of inquiry I'd like to pursue if you are sufficiently recovered from the ministrations of the Farling."

"I'm fine," Molly replied when the laughter subsided.

"I understand that you are the biological sister of Clive Oxford, the director of EarthCent Intelligence."

"That's true, but there's no connection between our relation and my captivity. I didn't even know I had a brother..." she trailed off.

"Didn't even know I had a brother," Jursha repeated for the floating immersive cameras. "Can you tell me how many Humans there are in our galaxy?"

"I don't suppose we exactly know anymore," Molly mumbled. "Around ten billion, maybe?"

"So as a scientist, you must know that the odds of your ever meeting a brother who you didn't even know existed would be…?"

"Around zero," Molly admitted.

"So if not for the Free Republic rescuing you from the defective vessel in which you were surveying Hevel Five, without a permit if I may add, you never would have been in a position to activate one of the few remaining VTGERN devices, which led directly to your encounter with a large beetle who collects humanoid genetic samples and who matched you with your unknown sibling!" Jursha declared triumphantly.

The entire room suddenly took on a brown tint from the cheerful faces of Hortens exchanging the alien equivalent of fist bumps, and Kelly found herself sinking lower in her chair while wishing that she had a desk to hide behind. Crute rose from his own seat and patted the air with all four arms in an attempt to calm the audience.

"Hortens Four, Humans Zero," he announced. "I see no reason to extend this hearing any longer." Then he moved forward and pushed to the front of the line to get an autograph from Jursha.

Seventeen

"This is embarrassing," Ambassador White declared. "I was finally getting used to the aliens calling us Stryx pets, but now they think that even the pirates are running some kind of charity for our benefit."

"I admit the Horten advocate was good," Kelly said, glancing around the holo-conference at the other members of the Intelligence Steering Committee. "If we had seen it coming, we could have prepared better and perhaps chosen different witnesses, but I didn't know there would be a cross-examination until it was under way."

"Perhaps the Stryx intended it as a lesson for us," President Beyer speculated. "I never realized how overly dependent I had become on our station librarian until I returned to Earth. They may have conjured up this whole crisis as a polite way to tell us to take responsibility for ourselves."

"Or to start growing up," Carlos Oshi, the Middle Station ambassador, corrected the president. "Although our local Verlock ambassador assures me that I am sadly deficient at statistical analysis, I can't believe that the review of our probationary status taking place at the same time as the policy reset on piracy is a coincidence."

"I got blindsided by the review feedback," Ambassador Zerakova said. "The frustrating thing is that colleagues I think of as my friends—they are my friends—had apparently been bottling this stuff up for years to save my feelings. All that time I thought that the Vergallians and the Grenouthians were looking for excuses to put us down, it turns out they thought they were going easy on us."

"I've collected and collated the responses from all of our ambassadors to Stryx stations and the pattern is crystal-clear," the Void Station ambassador spoke up. "With the exception of the Verlocks, who universally encouraged their human counterparts to study remedial mathematics, the feedback consisted almost entirely of complaints about the things that make us human."

"Maybe being bad at math *is* one of the things that makes us human, Zhao," the president commented.

"Once I got over the initial shock, I began to get the feeling they were all dancing around some larger issue," Kelly said.

"You mean they aren't really complaining about the way we flare our nostrils or how we slurp our soup?" Ambassador Fu asked.

"It's just that they were all so, I don't know, shifty about it. I can't help wondering if they know something we don't."

"They know lots of things we don't," the president observed. "Speaking of things we don't know, I was hoping you could get Mr. Oxford to participate in this meeting."

"He and his wife are waiting in the reception area outside my office," Kelly said. "They wanted to give us a chance to discuss the recent intelligence misses amongst ourselves before they join the holo-conference."

"You're referring to the piracy hearing?"

"Actually, they feel worse about the questions they suggested we use to prepare for our review meetings with the alien ambassadors."

"And well they should," Svetlana said. "I went into the meeting with the Horten ambassador on my station primed to talk about gaming and was told that we're litterbugs. And my Vergallian counterpart suggested that I find something to do with my hands while talking, rather than waving them around like I'm being attacked by flying insects."

"Arm-waving aside, I think it's well established by this point that the aliens don't see us as a threat to their economic well-being," the president continued. "Since there's nothing we can do about having tin ears and noisy digestive tracts, I suggest we concentrate on the areas where we can improve."

"Like no more singing 'Happy Birthday' with aliens in the room?" Belinda asked.

"That would be one possibility, but I was thinking more in terms of adding, rather than taking away. Who can tell me what all of the aliens doing business on Earth have in common?"

"They're oxygen-breathers," Ambassador Oshi replied immediately.

"Yes, there's that, but I meant something more fundamental."

"They're humanoids, and as such, the Stryx probably fiddled with their genes," Ambassador Fu said bluntly.

"I just learned that all of the oxygen-breathing tunnel network species independently developed their own version of the 'Alley Cat' dance," Kelly added. "The local Farling doctor implied that it's part of our genetic programming."

"Perhaps I should have been more specific," the president said patiently, sounding rather like a Stryx librarian

201

himself. "The aliens doing business on Earth are all contributing to our economy."

"They're on Earth to make money," Svetlana pointed out.

"And it works both ways." President Beyer looked around the virtual table, pausing for a moment on each ambassador. "What have we contributed to alien economies, other than low-cost labor?"

"InstaSitter," Kelly replied. "The Vergallian ambassador told me so herself."

"They only offer babysitting on the Stryx stations," Ambassador White reminded her.

"I'd say the Galactic Free Press, but I guess the only aliens who read it are spies," Kelly followed up on her first answer.

"Closer," the president said. "Can anybody tell me why?"

"I suppose that alien spies get paid for reading it," Ambassador Tamil suggested.

"Reporters are similar to tourists, Raj," the president explained. "They travel to alien worlds where they rent rooms, buy expensive synthesized meals, and hire local guides."

"But there are so few of them," Kelly objected. "How can one or two reporters visiting an alien world contribute to the economy?"

"They can't," the president agreed. "And there aren't enough human tourists or businessmen visiting alien worlds to have any noticeable impact either. There aren't enough of us and we don't have much money. I was just pointing out that tourism is one way humans could contribute to the economies of the tunnel network member worlds that allow visitors."

"Is this your idea or did you get it from consultants?" Ambassador Oshi asked suspiciously.

"Let me answer your question with another question. When you attend a party on Middle Station, what sorts of aliens do you meet?"

"All kinds, I suppose," Carlos said. "Well, diplomats mainly. If you take into account that the aliens are bothered by the way that we eat, smell, talk, drink and move, it's not surprising that most of our social contacts with other species are work related."

"As are my own contacts with aliens. But while your duties primarily bring you into contact with diplomats, my main job for the last several years has been making extraterrestrial entrepreneurs feel welcome on Earth," the president said. "I've learned that businessmen have a different way of seeing the galaxy than diplomats, which is why I've come to the conclusion that the EarthCent Intelligence 'miss' referred to earlier is the fault of this committee for steering them in the wrong direction. Could you invite Mr. and Mrs. Oxford to join us now, Kelly?"

During the brief delay while Clive and Blythe took their seats and were added to the hologram, the other ambassadors batted the president's thesis back and forth, trying to come up with any contributions that humans had made to alien economies. Raj brought up the sovereign human communities movement, which was adding to the trade of open worlds run by several friendly species. Svetlana reminded him that these were universally populated by ex-contract workers who had been screened by the aliens when they were hired and had chosen to stay after their terms were complete.

"They're still contributing," Ambassador White argued.

"True," the president allowed. "But you are talking about open worlds, which by definition are recently developed planets with low populations. I'd like to see us making visible contributions on established alien worlds, perhaps their homeworlds, if that's possible. Ah, Director Oxford. Thank you for joining us."

"I apologize for the prep questions we sent the ambassadors," Clive said immediately. "It was a poorly conceived idea on my part. I allowed my own preconceptions about the importance the aliens place on economics shape the instructions I gave to our analysts. If I had given them free rein, I'm sure the results would have been more useful."

"I don't believe anything could have prepared us for the feedback we received from our colleagues, and frankly, it wouldn't have made a difference even if we had known what they were going to say," Ambassador Oshi replied. "My Drazen friend criticized me for breathing through my mouth rather than my nose. How do you change something like that at my age?"

"No apology is required," the president told the Oxfords. "When the two of you took over our intelligence service, I had my doubts about the focus you put on business information, but I understood that you wanted the agency to be self-funding, so I didn't object. Now I see that your approach was correct all along, and that it would have made no sense for us to have spies running around trying to steal military secrets and causing diplomatic crises. Looking forward, my question is whether we have the potential to contribute directly to the economies of any of the alien homeworlds."

Clive deferred to his wife, who answered without hesitation. "Potential? Certainly. Capability? That's another matter. I'm assuming you wouldn't want to pursue the low hanging fruit."

"Such as?"

"I could stake any number of human merchants I know to open import/export businesses on alien worlds, but do we really want them competing with the native businesses or the manufacturers and exporters you've attracted to Earth? Besides, I thought you had to grant all of the alien businesses you brought in monopolies, even the Vergallian dance academy."

"Thank you for reminding me. Just because I talk with businessmen all the time now doesn't mean I've become one, and I'd completely forgotten about the guaranteed terms." The president made a little circling motion with his forefinger on his desk, like he was winding an old fashioned reel-to-reel tape recorder that held his memory before continuing. "Hildy tells me that our best use of resources would be to do something unique, since the visibility of the contribution is more important to our goal than the financial impact. It's too bad that 'Let's Make Friends' is actually a Grenouthian production."

"Could InstaSitter be extended to alien worlds?" Kelly asked.

"I wish," Blythe replied. "The reason InstaSitter only operates on the tunnel network stations is that we are totally dependent on the Stryx librarians for all of our back office support."

"You couldn't convince Libby to help out remotely, like she does with the teacher bots?"

"The aliens wouldn't tolerate it," Blythe said. "They depend on the Stryxnet for real time communications, the Stryx registers for certain financial transactions, and of course, they use the tunnels and ship controllers. But none of them would welcome a business that relied on direct Stryx involvement, and I'm sure Libby would decline for competitive reasons if I asked."

"You couldn't replicate your business model on alien worlds using the native technology for your infrastructure?"

"Not without being at a huge disadvantage on cost," the co-founder of InstaSitter explained. "Part of the reason we were able to succeed on the tunnel network is that we offer babysitting for all of the aliens using part-time employees from all of the species. On a Drazen world we'd be providing babysitting for Drazens using Drazen girls. Even if the business worked initially, the first well-funded local who came along and wanted to push us out could do so. On the stations, no species has an inherent advantage, and we discourage competition by operating on such thin margins that nobody wants to bother."

"But the idea was brilliant," the president insisted. "With all of the business data your agency is gathering, couldn't you come up with something similar for aliens? Some business that they've overlooked or abandoned so long ago that they've forgotten about it?"

"Like Dorothy," Kelly suggested. "SBJ Fashions started with her trolling through the lost-and-found for discarded styles."

"Then we should have drafted Daniel for this meeting, though now that I think of it, he's off visiting one of the members of his sovereign human communities," Blythe said. "I know that many of the humans on open worlds are providing sub-contracting services to the alien proprietors after completing their labor contracts. A product that works for a Dolly on a Dollnick open world might translate to one of their more established planets."

"I knew I was missing something obvious," the president said. "One of the most successful businesses on Earth is the floater factory operated by humans from Chianga under license from Prince Drume. It never occurred to me to ask the, uh, Chiangans, whether they had any ideas for opening businesses on Dollnick worlds rather than Earth."

"I realize we missed the first part of this meeting, Mr. President, but perhaps you can explain the connection between our intelligence failures and opening businesses on alien planets," Clive requested. "I can't imagine we would be making any significant economic contributions, and thanks to the Grenouthian documentaries and Aisha's show, I suspect most of the tunnel network aliens could already pick a human out of a police line-up."

"It's easy," Raj interjected. "We're the ugly Vergallians."

"Actually, I was saving that part of the explanation for when you joined this holo-conference, and then I forgot to give it," the president admitted. "Allow me to take a brief poll. After meeting with the ambassadors on your stations about the issues they have with humanity, how many of you asked what you could do to correct the situation?"

"But they weren't things we can correct!" Svetlana objected. "We already agreed on that."

"I promised the Verlock Ambassador I would look at the math book he gave me, but I gave up after five minutes," Kelly admitted.

"I talked to a meditation teacher about breathing through my nose," Ambassador Oshi volunteered. "She told me to try taping over my mouth."

"Earlier this evening, I attended a Grenouthian party in the city to celebrate their restoration of archival movie footage documenting cavalry charges in World War One," the president said. "They were positive it would be a blockbuster, but I digress. Most of the important alien businessmen on the North American continent were in attendance, so I took the bull by the horns and asked each of them how they cope with all of our unpleasant characteristics. Do you know what they said?"

"Nose filters and contact lenses," Kelly guessed, but the president ignored her.

"Every last one of them told me, and I quote, 'Oh, you get used to it.' And that made me question whether we are the only species on the tunnel network with disturbing odors and aggravating conversational styles."

"Did you bring that up with them?" Clive inquired.

"I did, and I got an earful, but it was all past tense. The Drazens used to be driven insane by the high-pitched whistling produced by the Dollnicks, and the Frunge wandered around in shock that everybody else used woody plants for construction materials. I don't have to tell you that the Verlocks drove everybody nuts with their slow speech. The Dollnicks still whistle, wood furniture is more popular than ever, and the Verlocks probably speak slower than they did a million years ago. The only thing that's changed is familiarity."

"But most of the aliens still live on their own worlds," Ambassador White pointed out. "It's not like they've all been mixed up for hundreds of thousands of years and developed some kind of genetic resistance."

"Not genetic, psychological," the president asserted. "When a Drazen meets a Dollnick in person for the first time, he knows that the Dolly isn't whistling on purpose to give him a headache. But when a human invites a member of another species to a party and sings 'Happy Birthday,' that alien wonders if we're being obnoxious on purpose."

"And you think that opening high profile businesses on their homeworlds will accelerate the process of habituating the other species to humanity?" Clive asked.

"I want to do something proactive and it's all I could come up with," the president replied. "It's going to be a long process no matter what we do, but it seems like a reasonable investment."

"We'll take a look at the data and see what we can come up with, but in my experience, creating businesses with an ulterior motive usually results in losing a lot of money," Blythe said.

"I'm just looking for a starting point, so that regular mom-and-pop aliens who never travel off-world will see, smell, and hear humans contributing something to their planetary economies. I want those aliens to learn that humans aren't just entertainment content."

"Perhaps a business like the Thark soap bars," Ambassador Fu suggested.

"I'm not sure that providing the Tharks with a semi-addictive intoxicating stimulant is our proudest hour," the president replied.

"I don't mean the soap itself, that's no different from exporting wine to the Frunge. But an enterprising woman here on Void Station who manufactures her own line of organic soaps opened a café for Tharks to come in and lick them. Anne has been successful enough to pick up two new competitors in the last cycle, but she still gets mad at me when I call them soap bars rather than cafés."

"The Tharks would never allow a human business on one of their worlds," Clive said. "Despite their deep integration in the tunnel network as financial middlemen, they keep their off-station lives strictly private."

"We don't currently have a Thark ambassador on Union Station, they don't seem to feel it's worth the bother," Kelly said. "Did anybody get feedback from one during the review?"

"Ironically, they complained about our hygiene," Ambassador Fu replied.

"Soap-based intoxicants aside, the concept is intriguing," President Beyer continued. "The Drazens will eat anything. Perhaps they would welcome a restaurant chain featuring human cuisine? It has the built-in advantage that the human employees would be part of the dining experience."

"I'll ask Herl for his opinion," Clive said. "He's on the station advising the Drazen ambassador on the piracy reset. I'll repeat your proposition word for word, and I'm sure the first thing he'll ask is whether you were proposing to put people on the menu."

Eighteen

"You know, you're different than you were when we were kids."

"I better be," Kevin replied to the ambassador's daughter. He dipped the roller in the deep end of the tray and then drew it up the ribbed slope to shed the excess paint. "We were seven years old then. Are you going to help, or are you going to play with Alexander all night."

"That's exactly what I mean," Dorothy said, showing no indication that she intended to abandon the puppy for a paintbrush. "You would never have said anything like that when you were seven. I think you were afraid I'd get mad and leave or something."

"Don't forget that I didn't go to school or get to meet many other kids, other than my older brothers and sisters. I probably thought that if I did something wrong you'd just go back to your Union Station friends." The roller left a horizontal swath of white paint on the blood-red bulkhead, and the young man began working it up and down to take out the drips. Then he squatted to reload the roller and looked over at Dorothy, who was sitting with her back against the opposite bulkhead and absently scratching behind the puppy's ears. "And I didn't develop a lot of new social skills living alone in a two-man ship. It's mainly exercise, reading, and watching immersives."

"But traders have great social skills," the girl protested. "How else could you barter with all those people and aliens?"

"Work is different," Kevin replied, applying another stripe of paint to the metal partition. "You do it because you have to, and after a while it becomes easy. I can swap dirty jokes with a Drazen that I'd be too embarrassed to ever tell a human."

"Then where did you learn them?"

"From other Drazens. It's kind of a thing with them."

"Tell me one."

"No way. Do you think you could grab that paintbrush and cut in along the deck?"

"I've never even seen a brush like that. Why aren't you using my dad's sprayer?"

"It would just get gummed up with this stuff. The paint is specially formulated to hide old colors in a single coat, and it's also supposed to encapsulate any microscopic spores that may have survived the vacuum," Kevin explained. "I was on a Sharf orbital a few years ago when they recovered a ship drifting in space that had a human crew. When they did the autopsies…"

"I don't want to hear about it," Dorothy interrupted, putting her hands over her ears and humming loudly until she saw that he had given up. Then she tried to push Alexander's head off of her lap without success and went back to stroking his soft fur. "I was going to help, but your dog won't let me."

"Alex," Kevin said in a stern voice. "Go find your brother and play."

The puppy rose, yawned, did a yoga stretch, and then trotted down the ramp and out of the modified scout ship. Dorothy looked after him for a moment, feeling a bit put out that Alexander had abandoned her so easily after all the attention she lavished on him, but that was the nature of the Cayl hounds after they chose a partner.

"So how does this work?" Dorothy asked, examining the paintbrush doubtfully.

"Dip the bristly end in the paint, clean off the excess on the edge of the tray so it doesn't drip all over the drop cloth, and then apply the paint to the areas that the roller can't reach."

"I think it's broken," the girl reported after a few minutes. "The paint isn't going on smoothly."

"You can't just poke with it," Kevin said in exasperation. "Hold the brush so that the bristles just reach the tape I put down, and then draw it along in smooth strokes. That's better, but you need more paint."

After working for around three minutes, Dorothy took a break and pondered out loud, "I wonder why the previous owner wanted everything red?"

"I suppose she liked red. I've never met any Kurdas, but maybe they came from a world with a red sun. Lots of species like interior colors that aren't shades of white. The habitat that Paul brought back for a house was all pale green inside when we found it."

"Aisha mentioned that there was some sort of stain bleeding through the paint that the Dollnicks used in one of the rooms. We should go over and look. I haven't even been on the top deck yet."

"That doesn't sound right," Kevin said, working the roller back and forth in the tray in an attempt to sponge up any remaining paint. "The Dollnicks probably know even more metal coatings than the Sharf."

"Why is that? Don't the Sharf build more ships?"

"The Sharf don't paint anything. They're into additives that create different color alloys. The only reason I'm familiar with painting at all is that the used Sharf ship I bought with a Stryx mortgage had a black interior. Believe it or not, whoever owned it before me had added little glow-in-the-dark stickers of stars and galaxies to every surface. I kept on floating into bulkheads and having nightmares that I was outside without a spacesuit. I had to go over it three times with Earth paint before the white stopped looking gray. The trader who was selling the stuff warned me I should have chosen the oil-based rather than the latex, but I'd never painted before, and the latex was supposed to be easier to clean up."

"Now that I think of it, I had to buy black polish from a Dollnick once, and he made it really complicated."

"Well, this paint will cover anything," Kevin continued, holding up the can as he tipped it over the roller tray and shook it in an effort to get another drop out. "You have to stir it up really good, because the thick stuff sinks to the bottom, and that's what creates the barrier. The instructions say to turn the can upside down and shake it for five minutes, but I just made sure that the cover was on tight, and then I let the dogs play with it until they got bored."

"You just used up the whole can to cover this bit of bulkhead?" Dorothy asked.

"That's because it goes on so thick. It's not just to cover the red and protect against flesh-eating fungi, you know. The Farling doctor suggested this paint because it blocks most harmful radiation. When I found out how much it cost, I almost got sick again. But when I complained to him about the price on my last visit, he told me how much he would have charged to fix up my radiation overdose if I had been paying out of pocket. All of a sudden, the paint seemed like a bargain."

"Do you get a lot of radiation in space?"

Kevin looked at her incredulously. "You really are a station brat, aren't you? Radiation is all that some traders talk about, like people back on Earth used to obsess about the weather. It depends on where you go and what kind of ship you're in. The colony ships and alien navies all use active shielding, so it's not an issue for them, but you don't get that kind of protection on a cheap trade vessel."

"Paul and Aisha don't need radiation shielding in the hold, but the paint might still be worth the price if the area they need to cover is small," the practical girl replied. "Let's go take a look at their stain."

"All right. I'm just going to step out of these coveralls since I'm done for the day." Kevin pulled down the zipper that ran from his collar to his waist, shrugged his arms out of the sleeves, and let the whole garment fall down around his ankles. Underneath he was wearing his usual jeans and a T-shirt. Then he kicked off his sandals, stepped out of the coveralls, and hung them over the stepladder.

"You aren't going to wash those? I could throw them in with our stuff."

"Coveralls? I didn't know anybody ever washed them, and anyway, I've only been wearing these since I started working with Paul and Joe."

"Ew." Dorothy clamped her thumb and forefinger over her nostrils, though the truth was she hadn't smelled anything.

"Let's go," Kevin said, stepping back into his sandals and heading down the ramp. "If this doesn't take too long, maybe we can go out and listen to some music or something. Anything other than that Horten band."

"They're actually really good," Dorothy protested, bumping repeatedly into the boy's side as they walked along until he finally got the idea to put his arm around her. "They were only playing those songs because Aisha invited all of the alien kids who have been on her cast."

"So what's with your brother and Vivian? I saw Molly and her son at the Farling's medical shop yesterday. They told me that she has a crush on Samuel, but he's in love with a Vergallian princess or something."

"Queen, actually, though she has a protector because she's too young to rule. She lived with us for a while when Aisha brought her home from the show after her Vergallian nurse abandoned her. Ailia used to follow Samuel around the way you used to follow me around," she teased. "I guess Jeeves must have fixed them up with some secret way to keep in touch, but my brother won't talk about it."

"And your parents don't discourage him?"

"They're just kids, you know, and Vergallians mature much slower than humans. I think Vivian has a whole strategy laid out for winning him. She even started taking fencing lessons when he's at work."

"I saw. She's scary good."

"She's scary good at everything, it runs in their family. Of course, Blythe was the same way about Paul and in the end she lost him to Aisha, but Vivian has the whole same-species thing working for her. Don't let any of them hear you talking about it, though. They all think it's a secret."

"Aunty Dorothy, Uncle Kevin," Fenna greeted the pair when they reached the newly-occupied habitat. "We have toilets now and everything. Did you come to look at the stain?"

"Yes, we did," the ambassador's daughter replied. "I hear it's in your bedroom."

"It's not my bedroom if the stain keeps getting blacker," the girl said, suddenly serious. "It's getting squarer too."

"Is that a word?" Dorothy asked.

"More square," Kevin translated. "It sounds like an interesting stain."

Fenna ran up the welded stairs that Joe had fabricated for accessing the upper decks, and Kevin and Dorothy followed at a more sedate pace. Aisha and Paul were busy on the second story rolling out new rugs purchased in the Shuk, but they waved off Kevin's offer to help.

"Go on up and take a look," Paul said. "Joe was pretty mad when he saw it. He headed over to the Dollnick repair facility right after supper to complain, but it's not worth emptying the house out and moving it back there to get one little area repainted."

"I was just helping Kevin paint and he has stuff that will cover over anything," Dorothy boasted. Then she sped up the second flight of stairs to catch up with him.

Fenna stood in the doorway of her room, unwilling to enter. "There," she said, pointing, though it would have been impossible for anybody to miss the source of her trepidation. "It's gotten a lot bigger and darker. And more squarer."

"That's not the old color bleeding through," Kevin observed. He walked right up to the blackening patch and crouched a little to get a closer look. "Fenna. Go and tell your father to come up here."

"I don't like it," Dorothy said. An unaccustomed wave of anxiety swept over her.

Kevin turned back to the girl and his eyes went wide. "What happened to your bracelet?"

217

Dorothy looked down and saw that the runes on her bracelet were glowing like the time an alien from the Cayl Empire came to the lost-and-found to kidnap her. But unlike the bracelet's reaction to the Lood, she could feel it thrumming with power, as if it were about to do something. "Get it off me," she croaked, finding herself paralyzed from the neck down.

Kevin grabbed her forearm with one hand and reached for the bracelet with the other, but his hand kept slipping off of some invisible shield and he couldn't get his fingers around the alien artifact.

Paul pounded into the room and swore out loud. "I just pinged Jeeves and he's on the way, but he's outside the station so it will be a few minutes."

"I'm going to carry her out of here," Kevin declared, and put his words into action, scooping Dorothy off of her feet. At that moment, there was a bright flash, and the section of bulkhead that had formerly been turning black suddenly disappeared altogether, revealing a figure lying on a narrow cot. Dorothy's rigid body relaxed, causing Kevin to almost drop her, and the runes on her bracelet rapidly faded to black.

"I'm all right," Dorothy said. "You can put me down, unless you don't want to. Libby? What's going on?"

"It seems that you have located the owner of the bracelet," the Stryx librarian observed dryly.

"But you said I could have it."

"After the bracelet went unclaimed in the lost-and-found for nearly six thousand years, it seemed like a reasonable course of action," Libby replied. "Gryph did warn me that the owner was likely just taking a nap somewhere, but the lost-and-found is my responsibility, and I can't keep things on the shelves forever."

Aisha arrived just in time for the last part of the station librarian's reply. "But Gryph included this habitat in the auction lot," she protested. "How can he sell something for salvage with the owner on board?"

"Even Teragram mages are responsible for parking fees," Libby explained. "Ah, she just pinged me for a language update. Perhaps she'll explain her presence."

Everybody turned to the humanoid figure on the cot who was just beginning to stir. The combination of feline facial features and bright feathers along the arms were reminiscent of an Egyptian goddess, but the most striking thing about the alien was the playful expression in her eyes.

"I am Baa," she declared in perfect English. "Take me to your leader."

"I'll get Mom," Dorothy offered, and fled the room without waiting for an answer.

"Don't go too far with my bracelet," Baa called after her. She swung her legs off of the cot, staying low to avoid bumping her head on the ceiling of the low compartment. After a brief pause, she rose unsteadily to her feet, supporting herself on the bulkhead. "Somebody painted over my entrance?"

"Badly," Paul said. "I'm beginning to suspect that my friend Jeeves, who is conspicuously absent, has involved us all in an elaborate practical joke."

"Jeeves is a Stryx?" Baa asked, offering a friendly feline smile to Fenna, who was peeking out from behind her father. "I expect the AI are displeased with my napping in long term parking without seeking permission. I understand from the station librarian that you have purchased my camper at an auction for unpaid parking bills. I do not object to the transaction as it clears my account with the Stryx at a considerable discount."

"Camper?" Fenna piped up.

"That is the closest term I can find in this new vocabulary. Based on our current location, I assume that you are repurposing my camper as a stationary domicile. Given its lack of integrated propulsion and active life support systems, you've chosen a reasonable application."

"You lived in a big empty box in space with nothing but partitions?" Kevin asked. "We thought it was an abandoned habitat that had been stripped."

"I intended to furnish it when the remittance I've been expecting arrives from home, but something seems to have delayed it."

"You've been in stasis over six thousand years waiting for a bank transfer?"

"I may have been overreacting to an adverse event in my personal life," Baa admitted. Dorothy reentered the room, followed closely by her mother, who was panting a little after the two flights of stairs. The mage must have already recovered from waking, because she stepped confidently away from the wall she had been using as a support and addressed Kelly. "Are you the official representative of this charming new species?"

"I'm the EarthCent Ambassador to Union Station."

"How convenient," Baa said, her cat-eyes sparkling with good humor.

"I, uh, I've studied for this," Kelly stuttered in frustration, straining to remember what came next without asking Libby for help. "As this is the first contact between our species, I want to assure you that our intentions are peaceful. We are members, I mean, probationary members, of the tunnel network, and if you aren't familiar with the Stryx, I would be happy to make an introduction."

"I see you're well versed in the first contact protocols," Baa complimented the ambassador. "My kind were present at the founding of the current tunnel network, though after examining the prospectus, we chose not to join. Aren't you going to ask about my intentions?"

"Right," Kelly said, giving herself a mental kick. "What are your intentions in initiating this contact?"

"I'm not sure I can be said to be the initiator," Baa mused. "The only immediate item on my agenda is to recover my bracelet, for which I will happily compensate the young lady as soon as my remittance arrives. Something to eat would be very nice as well."

"Do you think you can eat our food?" Kelly asked. "We've had supper already, but I haven't had time to put away the leftovers yet. You're welcome to come next door and see if there's anything that won't poison you."

"How kind of you," the mage replied, accepting her bracelet back from Dorothy. She held it up in front of her face and squinted at it critically. "Somebody has been fiddling with my multi-dimensional interface and I suspect a certain Stryx librarian. Is that your home, Ambassador?" Baa inquired, pointing out one of the large viewports at the ice harvester.

"Yes," Kelly replied. "It's nothing grand, but we have extra room if you need somewhere to stay."

A smile split the feline face almost in two. "An offer of food and an invitation to stay. What a wonderful species!" she added as if to herself, slipping the bracelet onto her wrist. "Now let's see if everything still works properly. Last one there is a rotten egg." A bright energy field enveloped Baa, and she vanished just as Jeeves floated into the room.

"I think you owe me an explanation," Paul said to his friend.

"About the sleeper?" the Stryx asked innocently. "I came across her entropy cocoon while I was checking the auction lot for Aisha. All of the other species who were interested in buying are biased against Teragram mages, perhaps for good reasons, so I couldn't say anything without ruining the price for Gryph. Besides, I thought it would make a nice surprise for the Ambassador. And if you get rid of the cot, it's a great space for shelves or built-in drawers."

"Why are so many species afraid of the Teragram mages?" Dorothy asked.

"They have a predilection towards playing gods to primitive cultures. The mythologies and histories of many of the tunnel network members record periods of Teragram influence or domination. They aren't at all malevolent, just fond of lounging around and accepting offerings. As long as you don't invite one for a meal or to stay in your home, you'll be fine."

Nineteen

"As this meeting room and the excellent catering were provided by the Stryx in order to facilitate our joint recommendation on the Humans, I believe we should make that our first item on the agenda. I also want to state for the record that my chairmanship of the piracy committee in no way extends to..."

"Enough, Crute," Czeros interrupted. "I'll chair the recommendation business if it means that much to you."

"Can I stay and listen?" Kelly asked. "I might learn something."

"The voting is confidential, Ambassador McAllister," the Frunge replied formally. "If you'll just wait in the corridor, I'll come and get you as soon as we're finished."

"All right, but I'm taking my tea and these cookies with me," Kelly retorted, placing her teacup on the cookie tray and rising from the table with both hands full. She walked slowly towards the exit, hoping to catch the beginning of the debate, but the alien ambassadors all remained uncharacteristically silent until the door slid shut behind her.

"Well, this is awkward," Bork exhaled, looking around at his colleagues. "Did anybody slip up and tell her the truth?"

"Does that mean you lied?" Srythlan rumbled.

"Well, I didn't go out of my way to upset her, though you wouldn't have known it from her reaction. What did you tell her?"

"I suggested that Human math skills are below par," Srythlan replied, looking down at the table.

"What a cop-out!" Bork declared. "You say that to everybody."

"She seemed surprisingly sincere in her desire for honest criticism," Abeva said. "I mentioned how most of them have terrible posture, and pointed out the difficulty in communicating with a species whose languages are so limited."

"But did any of you tell her about the real issue?" Bork persisted.

"Longevity?" The Horten ambassador who had reason enough to be disgusted with humanity for precipitating the piracy crisis shook his head. "That would just be cruel. By the time you get to know any of them, they're already forgetting your name and shuffling around like Verlocks."

"And losing their hair," the Gem ambassador added. "It's a mercy that it's much more prevalent with the males than the females."

"I feel a little guilty now about telling the EarthCent ambassador that they all speak without thinking," Crute admitted. "Did you hear that she's invited a Teragram mage to stay in her home?"

"What?"

"Oh, no!"

"Don't her Stryx friends tell her anything?"

"I only know about it because the Humans sent the mage's camper to one of our small ship repair facilities for rehab work," the Dollnick ambassador explained. "When the painter realized that there was a Teragram entropy cocoon active in one of the rooms, he panicked and painted over it without telling anybody. The manager of the shipyard only found out when the ambassador's husband came to complain that the paint was disintegrating."

"Poor Kelly," Czeros said, rubbing his jaw in concern.

"Maybe her artwork will drive the freeloader out," the Grenouthian ambassador suggested helpfully.

"The Human lack of impulse control is a symptom of the longevity issue," the Verlock ambassador said. "Their lives are so short that they are afraid to miss anything."

"But how does that explain the lazy ones?" the Chert ambassador inquired. "I've never seen a species with so many members who are willing to sit around and do nothing all day."

"They've become some of our best media content customers on a per capita basis," the Grenouthian ambassador said.

"So what do you all think?" Czeros coaxed his colleagues. "Why don't we just give them a pass and let them feel good about themselves for a change."

"That's another thing," Ortha complained. "They must be the most depressive species to hit the tunnel network since the Kasilians withdrew to go home and wait for death. You'd think they were actually responsible for some terrible event from the way they walk around looking guilty all the time."

"That's just one more reason to vote in favor," the Frunge ambassador said. "Can we make it unanimous?"

A chorus of "Ayes," came from around the table, and Czeros nodded in satisfaction. "Thank you. I will fetch the ambassador and give her the good news. You're it, Crute."

"Very well," the Dollnick said. "While we are waiting for our Frunge and Human members to return, I'll just say

225

that if I'm ever accused of a crime, I want Advocate Jursha to defend me."

"Our news network has been raking it in rerunning the hearing all over the galaxy," the Grenouthian ambassador boasted. "It couldn't have played any better if it had been scripted."

"Are you accusing us of something?" the Horten ambassador demanded.

"Lighten up, Ortha. He was giving Jursha a compliment," Bork said. "Now let's drop it or we'll kill Kelly's good mood."

The EarthCent ambassador was glowing like a Horten when she reached the table, and over Crute's objection, she insisted on going around to each ambassador and thanking them personally and effusively.

"You're starting to make me regret my vote," Abeva told her coldly.

"I know you don't really mean that," Kelly gushed. "And I want to take a moment to invite everybody to my home to meet our new guest. The Stryx tell me that it's been quite a while since there was a Teragram mage living on the station."

"Pass," Czeros said immediately, followed by every other ambassador with the exception of the Verlock, who just looked sad.

"On to the business at hand," Crute announced. "Stryx Jeeves will be arriving shortly to hear our proposal, so we don't have any more time to waste. Did your people complete the calculations, Srythlan?"

"The sum is manageable," the Verlock pronounced slowly. He opened a valise and began laboriously passing out thin sheets of a crystalline mineral packed with data and numbers. The Grenouthian ambassador waited about two seconds before seizing the whole stack and then hopping around the table to deliver them himself.

"What's this?" Kelly whispered to Bork, as she stared at the mass of alien symbols.

The Drazen looked over at her sheet, swiped his thumb along the top, and tapped on "Humanese." All of the text and numbers immediately converted to English.

"As you can see, we have provided cost projections for reducing piracy in decrements of five percent, starting from the thirty percent reduction level down to a seventy percent reduction," Srythlan explained.

"Why start at thirty percent?" Crute asked. "I thought the Stryx wouldn't settle for anything less than a fifty percent decrease."

"Thirty percent reflects the reduction in piratical activity we anticipate if all of the Gem exit the profession, and Hortens with more than two hundred years of service accept a buyout. If you'll give your attention to the cost/benefit curve in Figure 1, you'll see that our expenses accelerate rapidly if we are compelled to pay severance bonuses to younger pirates."

"I don't see a separate table for buying out my sisters," the newly appointed Gem ambassador said. "Surely you don't expect young clones to accept the same package as old Hortens?"

"There's an additional block grant to the New Gem Empire for reabsorption expenses in the miscellaneous footnotes."

"Have you included a calculation for savings from the reduction in piracy?" the Horten ambassador demanded.

"Illusory, for most of us," the Verlock replied. "The pirates have been careful to avoid creating large expenses for tunnel network species that would bring about a military response. Humans excepted," he added apologetically.

"So what exactly were the expenses that Jeeves was talking about when he said that the Stryx have had enough?" Crute asked. "As expensive as reactivating the VTGERN network for a single use must have been, that was just the one incident."

"I requested an accounting from the station librarian and the data was quite illuminating," Srythlan replied. "If you'll all proceed to the next page."

Bork reached over and tapped the center of Kelly's crystalline sheet at the bottom, bringing up a new set of tables and graphs.

"What is this?" Ortha frowned as he ran his finger along the table headings. "It looks like an enormous travel agency bill for a package vacation, complete with hotel rooms, transport and a meals allowance. But who includes clothing in a tour?"

"Safaris?" Czeros suggested.

"It's the expenses the Stryx have laid out for survivors of piracy attacks," the Verlock ambassador said. "While the AI don't interfere with piracy outside of the tunnel network, they see a steady flow of victims, including those who escape or abandon ship and make their way to a station after being attacked. As you can see, it's a substantial amount."

"Is my sheet translating the decimal place correctly?" Kelly whispered to Bork. "I'm afraid to bring up math in front of Srythlan, but I think that number is in the trillions."

"It is," the Drazen ambassador whispered back after consulting his own sheet. "Keep in mind it's a cumulative bill that's been adding up since your fascinating Ice Ages."

"Are you feeling well, Ortha?" the Chert ambassador inquired.

Kelly looked over and saw that the Horten had turned bright purple, and was trying unsuccessfully to hide his face with his hands, which were now a slightly darker shade of the same color. Czeros nudged the EarthCent ambassador and muttered, "Purple for embarrassment," and then continued in a louder voice, "I don't understand the probability projection you're making here, Srythlan."

For once, all of the ambassadors breathed a welcome sigh of relief when the Verlock began a ponderous explanation of the factors involved in predicting recidivism. Everyone kept their eyes studiously on their crystal sheets while Srythlan talked, even Kelly, who lost track of the proof immediately after the Verlock declared, "First, it is given that..." By the time that Srythlan finally reached, "Therefore, it is obvious...," Ortha was almost fully recovered, and Jeeves had floated silently into the room and taken his place at the opposite end of the table.

"I took a look at your proof, Srythlan, and I don't see that the conclusion is obvious at all," the Stryx said. "However, I'm less concerned with predictions about the behavior of future generations of pirates than what you intend to do in the next few cycles."

"I didn't know," Ortha suddenly said without explanation, but it was immediately clear to the other ambassadors what he was talking about. "I will need to contact my government again before making an official offer, but it is my belief that we should reimburse the Stryx for the expenses they have incurred in this vein."

"We're talking about a substantial amount of creds," the Grenouthian ambassador observed. "I believe it would be cheaper for all of us to go with one of the options presented by our esteemed Verlock colleague, provided the Stryx find that acceptable."

"Reimbursement does have the attraction of being computationally trivial," Czeros pointed out. "We've already agreed on how the costs will be shared by our species, so the only remaining challenge is to negotiate the amount with the Stryx. A straight cash payment offers a much cleaner solution than retraining programs with a requirement to monitor tens of millions of retired pirates to make sure they stay retired."

"I wish to state for the record that my chairmanship of this committee is concluded when the Stryx accept our solution..." Crute hastened to say, but the Horten ambassador interrupted the Dollnick before he could complete his disavowal of future responsibility.

"You didn't understand me," Ortha continued sadly. "I intend to request that my government repay the Stryx the full amount, which in the end will come down to a handful of creds per Horten citizen. I imagine this spells the end of my diplomatic career, but we are an honorable people. Will that be acceptable?" he asked, turning to face Jeeves.

"It's not my preferred solution, but it meets our requirements," the Stryx replied.

"How will that reduce piracy?" Kelly blurted out before she could stop herself.

"My people have been remiss when it comes to discouraging the less desirable elements in our society from leaving and taking up a, uh, less conventional lifestyle," the Horten ambassador replied in a tired voice. "Perhaps the imposition of a special tax assessment, even a small one, will lead families and employers to make a greater effort to rehabilitate those who go astray."

"What about a severance package for my sisters?" the Gem ambassador demanded of the Stryx.

"If Ambassador Ortha's proposal is accepted by his government, the Gem pirates will be free to remain in their current occupation," Jeeves replied.

"That makes no sense at all!" Kelly objected, "Here you have the chance to reduce piracy by between thirty and seventy percent, and instead you're willing to settle for a few trillion creds that Gryph probably earns from Union Station rents every year?"

"I think you're forgetting who is making the decision here, Ambassador," the Stryx replied. "If my elders felt that piracy was a threat to either the tunnel network or to the agreements we have made with other governing bodies, we wouldn't be here talking about costs. But it is not our way to interfere with the affairs of biologicals any more than necessary, and if your colleagues prefer Ambassador Ortha's offer over the option of reducing piracy through military action or financial incentives, that is their right. You have to admit that Advocate Jursha made a compelling argument."

"Hear, hear," a number of the ambassadors concurred, primarily in an attempt to cheer up their Horten colleague.

"So there's nothing further to discuss until Ambassador Ortha contacts his government," Crute declared. "I motion we close this meeting with the understanding that a positive response from the Hortens means that this committee is dissolved."

"Aren't we at least going to vote?" the Gem ambassador asked in frustration. "I never got to vote on anything other than the Human review!"

"I understand your disappointment, but as committee chairman, I can't ask members to potentially burden their

231

own governments with costs that the Hortens may be willing to shoulder alone," Crute replied. "None of us were in favor of military action, at least, none of us with militaries," he amended himself, glancing in Kelly's direction. "Under the proposed solution, the New Gem Empire will be free to spend the money you would have contributed to a joint fund on repatriating your own people."

"Second the motion," Abeva said.

"Third," Ortha muttered.

"All in favor? Carried." With that, Crute rose from the table and headed for the exit, quickly followed by most of the other ambassadors. Srythlan remained behind, engaged in some sort of complex calculations, and Kelly lingered in order to talk with Jeeves.

"Is this about your houseguest?" the Stryx asked the EarthCent ambassador. "I thought you'd be pleased with the opportunity to add another first contact to your resume."

"No, I—what do you mean 'another?'" Kelly demanded in response. "Wait. Are you hinting that I need a resume for some reason?"

"Your trip to Kasil was a first contact for Humans, as was Maker Dring. It's possible that some of the Cayl Empire species also had their first official contact with humanity through your embassy, though it's not something we keep track of. And I was using the resume as a figure of speech."

"You're just trying to get me confused by changing the subject. How can you defend piracy as a way of life?"

"We aren't defending piracy," Jeeves replied patiently. "We're defending your rights as members of our tunnel network to make your own choices, including bad ones, as long as they don't violate the rights of other species."

"But how about the people who have been attacked, held hostage, or killed by pirates. What about their rights?"

"And what about the criminal who sold the condemned ship Clive's sister ended up with? Should we police the used spaceship business everywhere on the tunnel network? Should I go to Earth and fly around intervening in violent crimes like some kind of comic book superhero?"

"But organized piracy…" Kelly began to object.

"The organized pirates are less of a problem than the rogues. I would have preferred if the ambassadors had reached a consensus to reduce the number of pirates, though as was pointed out, I expect that most of the clones have had enough of that lifestyle. As long as the New Gem Empire grants them an unconditional pardon and resettlement help, I predict that they will return to the fold."

"I don't understand. We could all see how ashamed Ortha was when he found out that the Stryx have been cleaning up after a Horten mess. Why didn't you give them a bill tens of thousands of years ago?"

"I wasn't alive tens of thousands of years ago," Jeeves reminded the ambassador. "But I think that the answer you are looking for is that the other members of the tunnel network never asked us to act. They all suspect that we are using the VTGERN activation as an excuse to interfere, and there's a good deal of truth to their suspicions."

"So now you're saying I don't understand any of the other species!"

"You have been going around begging for criticism," the Stryx pointed out. "I think you sometimes forget that the other ambassadors aren't really humans with odd bits and pieces tacked on. If anything, it works the other way around."

"Look here, Jeeves," the Verlock ambassador interrupted, shoving over a tablet packed with dense mathematical notations. "I've rechecked the equations for our recidivism projections and it turns out that the solution is obvious after all!"

"I was just having you on," the Stryx replied, poking the thick-skinned Verlock ambassador with his pincer.

Twenty

"Are you sure you don't want to come along?" Kelly asked her Teragram houseguest. "I thought you said that you've never seen a newborn human."

"I was stating a fact, not an ambition," Baa replied from her position on the couch. "Besides, I have thousands of years of dramas to catch up on."

"Dring is coming with me," the EarthCent ambassador coaxed the alien. "I know you want to meet him."

"All the more reason I should remain here so he knows where to find me. Do be a dear and bring me one of those delicious bubbly beverages your husband makes in the cellar."

"Beer," Kelly told her for at least the third time, accepting Baa's empty mug and heading downstairs. "And it's a lower deck, not a cellar."

As the ambassador drew a fresh pint from the keg, Libby inquired privately, "Is your guest getting on your nerves already?"

"She's almost as bad as Dorothy was after David left," Kelly complained. "I take that back. She's much more animated than Dorothy was, and she's kind of interesting to talk to, though I have difficulty following her. Are you sure she's fully recovered from the entropy thing? I can't even get her out to look around Mac's Bones or visit Dring's gravity surfer."

"Teragram mages are a bit like the vampires of your legends," Libby explained. "They won't enter a house unless you offer them food and invite them in."

"What does that have to do with it?"

"Knowing that they are unlikely to receive a second invitation when the first one wears out, they can be reluctant to leave. I believe the record for a tunnel network species playing host to a Teragram mage was over a hundred generations for the Verlock royal family."

"You mean the mage stayed inside as a houseguest for thousands of years?"

"Several hundred thousand years," the station librarian replied. "Verlocks are excellent hosts and slow breeders."

Kelly retraced her steps with the refilled mug, accepted Baa's thanks, and headed out to meet Dring. The Maker had almost reached the ice harvester by the time Kelly got to the bottom of the ramp, and the two of them made their way towards the lift tube.

"Do you have any experience with Teragram mages as guests?" Kelly asked him.

"We dare not trust our wit for making our house pleasant to our friend, so we buy ice cream," Dring responded.

It took Kelly a moment to realize that the Maker was testing her with a quote. "Don't tell me," she said, closing her eyes in concentration. "Not an English author, right? Not even a novelist?"

"Correct."

"But it's from my library."

"It's from your shelves," Dring hedged. "I've noticed that Joe's taste in books is less romantic than your own."

"Thoreau?" she hazarded a guess.

"Very close. Ralph Waldo Emerson."

"American authors it is, then," Kelly said, and challenged the Maker with a quote of her own. "I believe that on the first night I went to Gatsby's house, I was one of the few guests who had actually been invited."

Dring came to an abrupt halt in front of the lift tube and gave his friend a searching look of concern.

"I did it again, didn't I?" Kelly let out her breath like a deflating balloon. "I gave you the title in the quote. Do you think my mind is going already? My mom is still sharp as a tack and I hoped I'd take after her."

"It's impressive that you could recall an American quote related to guests at all," Dring comforted her. "I was sure you'd go with an old standby from Benjamin Franklin."

"I can't get used to the fact that most of the alien ambassadors I know were alive at the same time as Franklin," Kelly responded, hoping to cover up the fact that she couldn't recall the famous saying in question. "Some of them were even serving on Union Station when Franklin was writing his autobiography."

"Lynx and Woojin's house," Dring told the lift tube as they stepped inside. "What you lack in longevity you make up for in fertility. It all works out the same in the end, except for it being different individuals."

"That seems like a pretty big difference to me," Kelly objected. "The concept sounds familiar, though. Is it from the Higher Determinism belief system that Dorothy's Vergallian friend tried explaining to me?"

"They just copied it from us," the Maker replied. When the capsule stopped, he politely ushered Kelly out into the corridor. "I've only been here once before. Which way is it?"

"Stop trying to make me feel good," the ambassador said, but she couldn't help smiling as Dring pretended to be perplexed over the location of Lynx's apartment. "It's two corridors down and then the, uh, the fifth door on the left."

Three corridors down at the fourth door on the right, Kelly located the right apartment by reading the nameplate. She touched the lock pad and the door slid open.

"No question about your being welcome here as a guest," Dring told her.

"We're in the other room," Woojin's voice called. "Is that you, Kelly?"

"Yes," the ambassador replied, heading for the bedroom with the Maker in tow. Lynx was sitting up in bed, looking wan but happy, and her husband was holding the baby like it was a hot piece of delicate crystal that he was simultaneously terrified of dropping or crushing.

"Do you know anything about this burping stuff?" Woojin asked. "No manual included."

"I just patted mine on the back, maybe bounced and rubbed a little, but I didn't bottle feed, and neither of them were big burpers. Didn't the midwife go over this with you, Lynx?"

"Wooj likes to ask everybody who visits," Lynx said. "I've never seen such a nervous man."

The ex-mercenary stood ramrod straight with the baby held against his shoulder, bouncing gently on his heels and patting like he was shaping a hamburger. "Just make sure you're supporting his head, Woojin." Kelly added.

"You haven't heard?" Lynx asked, breaking out in an enormous grin. "The Farling got it wrong."

"I told you that watch was just a gag gift."

"Not the watch. My delivery time was just two minutes late and I won the bet. But our baby is a girl."

"A girl? What did the doctor say when he found out?"

"Oh, you know Farlings. He said something critical about our chromosomes and implied that he wasn't really paying attention because it's all too primitive to hold his interest."

"You look quite happy with the outcome," Dring commented.

"I am. I always wanted a girl, and Woojin actually kept telling me that we would have one based on my dreams. Plus, the doctor visited this morning and returned double his fee!"

"We're not keeping the money, Lynx," her husband said sternly. "I would happily pay him ten times what he charged."

"I know, I know. I just want to make the beetle sweat it out for a few days."

"So what's her name?" Kelly asked.

"Em," Lynx announced, beaming at her infant.

"For Emma? Emily?" the ambassador guessed.

"M793qK," the new mother replied. "I'm never going to let the Farling live his mistake down. Besides, it will give me a chance to tell the story about how I won fifty creds whenever somebody asks who she's named after. I just wish he had a waiting room so I could tell his other patients when I bring her in for immunizations."

"You're sticking with him as your pediatrician?"

"He got us this far, and she is perfect. We counted her toes and everything. If she gets any more beautiful, I'll have to hide her face with that ugly mask that Dorothy's Vergallian friend gave me."

Woojin returned the infant to her mother, and said, "Visiting hour is up. The midwife said five minutes maximum per customer. Lynx is supposed to be resting."

239

"You're worse than a mother hen," his wife grumbled, but she didn't protest further. Kelly and Dring offered their congratulations again and headed back to the lift tube.

"Would you like to come over and meet our new houseguest now, Dring?" Kelly offered. "She's very interesting and I think you have a lot in common."

The Maker halted and stared at the ambassador for the second time that morning. "Should I assume you mean that in the sense of shared experience and longevity, or are you hinting that I've overstayed my welcome in Mac's Bones?"

"Silly," Kelly said, borrowing her daughter's favorite expression. "I just meant that both of you have been so many places and seen so many things. Baa must be the only sentient on the station who doesn't seem like an infant to you, aside from Gryph, I mean."

"The Teragram mages are long-lived compared to the tunnel network species, though it's hard to pin down their lifespan as they spend thousands of years at a time in entropy cocoons. Much of their technology is focused on nanobots, and they are able to effect repairs to their bodies at the cellular level, not entirely unlike what we shape-shifters do as a natural process."

"Mac's Bones," Kelly instructed the lift tube as the door slid shut behind them. "She did some kind of dematerialization thing right in front of us. I've never even heard of that outside of science fiction."

"I'm sure you've seen the Cherts disappear in front of your eyes more than once."

"But they use those shoulder projectors to fool the eyes." The door opened and Kelly exited the lift tube along with the Maker. "Are you saying that she didn't really dematerialize? She just turned invisible and snuck past us?"

"The Teragram mages have more tricks up their sleeves than any other species I have encountered. Deception and misdirection are their stock in trade, in part because their numbers are too few to accomplish anything by force. Their civilization reached its peak tens of millions of years ago, but an increasing tendency towards complete independence from one another prevented them from achieving stability, and their population went into a steep decline. They would have gone extinct altogether if some of their number hadn't stumbled into the occupation of playing gods together on primitive planets."

"And the Stryx allow it?"

"On the balance the mages do more good than harm. I'm not aware of a single case where a species they took under active management failed to reach the next level of development."

"What comes after accepting alien techno-mages as gods?"

"Generally a loss of faith in pantheons and a shift to monotheism," Dring replied.

"Why does the galaxy have to be so weird?" Kelly complained, and then shouted, "Down," at the remaining unnamed puppy, who practically knocked her over with his enthusiastic greeting.

"Kelly," the Stryx librarian spoke over the ambassador's implant. "The results of our review are in."

"You can tell me out loud. I don't have any secrets from Dring."

"Humans will continue on probationary status for the foreseeable future," Libby announced, her voice echoing through the hold. Then she added at her normal volume,

"That was an all stations public address announcement, so don't worry that you have to tell anybody."

"We failed? What are we doing wrong? Was it all the alien criticism?"

"No, the tunnel network ambassadors on all of the stations voted unanimously to welcome you into full membership. It's simply that you haven't met the criteria of developing your own faster-than-light drive and establishing a workable system of governance for your homeworld."

"But you knew that before the review started!"

"These things take place on a schedule," Libby replied evasively.

"What schedule? When's the next review?"

"I'm afraid that information will only be available when you come off of probation."

"I had to go through listening to all of my friends criticize me for nothing?" Kelly demanded.

"I hope it wasn't for nothing. And I do have some good news for you on the home front," the station librarian added, as Kelly and Dring approached the ice harvester. "Baa's remittance came in."

"But the other ambassadors told me that she was making it up. They said that the Teragram mages who visit your stations always talk about waiting for a remittance, and then they hang around eating you out of house and home."

"Jeeves is on his way to deliver it right now."

"This I'd like to see," the Maker said. "I've never heard of a Teragram mage actually receiving a remittance. Normally they dig in their heels until they hear about an employment opportunity in the god market."

242

The pair reached the ice harvester just as Joe, Paul and Kevin emerged after their morning coffee break. "What happened to you, Kevin?" Kelly asked. She tried to keep a straight face, but found herself unable to hold in her laughter.

"That's it," the young man declared, turning around on the ramp. "I'm not wearing this."

"You promised my daughter," Joe said, blocking Kevin's way back into the ice harvester. "Besides, I'm curious to see how the big pocket in the front works out. I saw a Grenouthian mechanic at work once, and you can keep a lot of tools handy in a belly pouch."

"Nobody laughs at giant bunnies," Kevin pointed out.

"Dorothy ambushed him during our coffee break," Paul explained to Kelly and Dring. "She's working on a new line for traders and she has a whole branding theme planned. What was it again?" he prompted Kevin.

"I.M.P.," the embarrassed young man replied, displaying the little imp embroidered above the breast pocket. "It stands for 'Improved Mobility and Protection.'"

"Spin around," Kelly ordered, and Kevin complied good-naturedly. "Have you ever seen anybody else wearing a green jumpsuit with shoulder boards?"

"Jeeves suggested I start using green fabric for prototypes because it's cheap," Dorothy explained, coming out of the ice harvester and slipping past her father and Paul. "The shoulder boards aren't just for aesthetics. They protect the wearer from, uh, shoulder injuries. I'm going to work with them to observe. So how are Lynx and the baby doing?"

"They're both fine," the ambassador replied. "And I haven't forgotten that you still owe me five creds from betting on Lynx's delivery time at the baby shower."

Dorothy suddenly became very interested in adjusting the angle of one of Kevin's shoulder boards in an effort not to see her mother's outstretched palm as she passed it. While Kelly and Dring waited for the ramp to clear, Samuel and Vivian appeared from the direction of the training camp. The two young teens were carrying fencing gear and arguing about something.

"It only counts if you get me with the tip," Samuel reiterated. "And the time you got me in the side was only because I was still extended from scoring on you, so it would have been waved off."

"That's dumb," Vivian said. "Who doesn't use the edge of a blade in a duel? And I only let you graze my side to create an opening. If we were really fighting, you would have been dead at least three times to my one!"

"But the Vergallian rules…"

"Do you see any Vergallians?" Vivian demanded, making a show of looking around the hold. "Does anybody see any Vergallians?"

"She's a tough one," Dring whispered to Kelly. "Do you think he knows what she's doing?"

"They're both still children," the ambassador whispered back, drawing a skeptical look from the Maker.

"Hey, Mom, Dring," Samuel said, finally noticing that they had an audience. "How's Lynx's baby?"

"She's a beautiful girl," Kelly replied. "Well, a bit red and wrinkly at the moment, but they all start like that."

"Cool. I've got work after dance practice today, so I'm going to eat with the Oxfords rather than coming all the way home. And Nigel will be by later to see if the last puppy wants to go with him and Vivian's aunt Molly."

"They're leaving already?"

"My dad rented a ship for his sister to finish her survey contract," Vivian answered. "She says the job is mainly done, and the work is just visiting a bunch of dead worlds and taking pictures from orbit, so they won't be gone for more than a few cycles."

Jeeves arrived, the lights on his case twinkling in a display of humor. "Did you see Kevin's shoulders?" the Stryx asked. "If I still worked for Libby's dating service, I'd say that any man who would wear something like that for a girl is a goner."

"That's my daughter you're talking about," Kelly said in a show of indignation. After confirming that Samuel and Vivian had continued on inside, she added, "Are you sure? I can never tell what she's thinking."

"Would you like to place a small wager?" Jeeves asked.

"Enough with the bets, already. I thought that the reason the Stryx opened Earth to start with was because we ran our economy like a casino."

"You ran your economy like a crooked casino," Jeeves corrected her. "There's a difference. Are you here to witness my punishment, Dring?"

"I suspected it might be something like that," the Maker replied with a toothy smile. "Shall we?"

The three made their way into the living room area of the ice harvester where Baa was sitting upright in a narrow space at the end of the couch. She was scowling at Beowulf, who had apparently asserted his property rights.

"My closest Human friend, a Maker and a Stryx," the mage said, rising to her feet and wiping her nose with one of Kelly's tissues. Beowulf immediately stretched out a little further, taking up the vacant space. "To what do I owe this visit to my temporary home?"

Jeeves extended his pincer to present the Teragram with an ornate box. She eagerly accepted the gift, opened the lid, and stared at the programmable cred resting on a velvet-like substance.

"Are you proposing, Jeeves?" Samuel asked. He already was on his way back out with Vivian, both of them having stored their fencing gear in the boy's room.

"In a manner of speaking," the Stryx replied, though the kids didn't even slow down for an answer as they passed. "Is this the remittance you were waiting for, Baa?"

"Oh, yes," she purred. "This will set me up just fine."

"Where did it come from?" Kelly asked.

"Wherever remittances usually come from, I imagine," the mage replied happily. "Who cares? I'd love to stay and chat, but I have quite a bit of shopping to do before I leave the tunnel network. These high-value programmable creds positively erode in value if you don't spend the balance quickly. You've been a lovely host, Ambassador, but I'm afraid I'm allergic to your dog so I won't be able to return." Upon concluding her speech, she swept out of the ice harvester without a backwards glance.

"Allergic to Beowulf?" Jeeves thundered.

"You didn't know?" Libby countered. "I doubt she would have lasted another day."

"That was half of my savings!"

"And I hope you learned a valuable lesson about dumping guests on unsuspecting friends," the Stryx librarian retorted. "Fish and visitors stink after three days."

"Benjamin Franklin," Kelly cried triumphantly. "Poor Richard's Almanac."

"Actually," Jeeves began, but seeing Dring shaking his head, he shifted gears and declared, "You're correct." If the Maker didn't want the EarthCent Ambassador to know where the saying had truly originated nearly a hundred million years earlier, the young Stryx had no objection.

EarthCent Ambassador Series:

Date Night on Union Station

Alien Night on Union Station

High Priest on Union Station

Spy Night on Union Station

Carnival on Union Station

Wanderers on Union Station

Vacation on Union Station

Guest Night on Union Station

Word Night on Union Station

Party Night on Union Station

Review Night on Union Station

Family Night on Union Station

Book Night on Union Station

LARP Night on Union Station

About the Author

E. M. Foner lives in Northampton, MA with an imaginary German Shepherd who's been trained to bite bankers. The author welcomes reader comments at e_foner@yahoo.com.

You can sign up for new book announcements on the author's website - IfItBreaks.com

Lightning Source UK Ltd.
Milton Keynes UK
UKHW03f1150300318
320279UK00001B/296/P